PLAZA
REQUIEM

PLAZA REQUIEM

STORIES AT THE EDGE OF ORDINARY LIVES

MARTHA BÁTIZ

Publishers of Singular
Fiction, Poetry, Nonfiction, Translation, Drama and Graphic Books

Library and Archives Canada Cataloguing in Publication

Bátiz, Martha, author
Plaza requiem : stories at the edge of ordinary lives / Martha Bátiz.

Issued in print and electronic formats.
ISBN 978-1-55096-682-4 (softcover).--ISBN 978-1-55096-683-1 (EPUB).--
ISBN 978-1-55096-684-8 (Kindle).--ISBN 978-1-55096-685-5 (PDF)

I. Title.

PS8603.A856P53 2017   C813'.6   C2017-905881-9
C2017-905882-7

Published by Exile Editions ~ www.ExileEditions.com
Printed and Bound in Canada by Marquis.

These stories are works of fiction. Names, characters, places and incidents
either are the product of the author's imagination or are used fictitiously.

We gratefully acknowledge the Canada Council for the Arts,
the Government of Canada, the Ontario Arts Council,
and the Ontario Media Development Corporation
for their support toward our publishing activities.

Canadian sales representation:
The Canadian Manda Group, 664 Annette Street,
Toronto ON M6S 2C8   www.mandagroup.com   416 516 0911

North American and international distribution, and U.S. sales:
Independent Publishers Group, 814 North Franklin Street,
Chicago IL 60610   www.ipgbook.com   toll free: 1 800 888 4741

For Edgar

"There, in each one of my actions,
I always find the enemy: the I,
The Fascist from within,
The dragon or the sea urchin whose insatiable mouth
Can only pronounce verbs:
I want, I devour, give me, move out of my way, revere me."

—José Emilio Pacheco, The enemy

PATERNITY, REVISITED

For Eduardo Pavlovsky

White and blue flag, blue and white sky. It's a sunny, crisp, spring morning that smells of cut grass and newborn flowers. Sunday. The surface of the river sparkles like satin with sequin embroidery. The Río de la Plata is bigger than she remembers; it's dark, and endless, like the sorrow it was forced to keep secret years ago. The park has not changed and, apparently, neither have his habits because he's right there, where she was expecting to find him. Where they used to sit every Sunday morning to watch boats drift down the river, eating *medias lunas* and sipping *mate.*

She fights the urge to turn back and run away. Her body has always been wiser than herself. It has made her vomit or has blinded her with headaches when she's needed to escape from certain moments. An ingrown toenail, she once read, means that you're not ready to move on with your life. She's always paid attention to the aches and pains in her feet. As if to punish them for knowing her better than she knows herself, she'd spent most of the previous evening trimming around her toenails until they bled – cutting a bit of skin here, a piece of nail there, digging deep into the flesh. Now the bandages are bulky under her well-worn running shoes; walking is painful, and she's forced to let her weight fall on her heels. Everyone must be thinking she walks funny, like a duck. What would they say if they knew why she's here? That small boy riding a bike with his father running close behind him; the woman pushing a stroller; those young people jogging...

The man is sitting on their bench, his back turned against her. She can still leave, but why bother coming all this way only to give up at the most crucial moment? She takes a deep breath and small, careful steps toward the all-too-familiar bench. Stopping a couple of feet behind him, she examines his thick, silver hair. It used to be dark brown, and she remembers it being soft. But not as soft as hers used to be. What if she swung her weighted bag now, like a mace, crushing his skull? One swift, precise movement, an impulse stemming from the depth of her fury. Her purse is heavy on her right shoulder so she switches it to the left, and looks around. Is anyone watching? Just then, the wind blows her way and the smell of his cologne hits her. She's eight again, longing for his embrace – and she freezes. How can her body be such a traitor? And then, as if this were a conspiracy, her shadow betrays her, too, and he turns around. When their eyes meet, he lets out a faint cry.

"Adriana!"

Taken by surprise, she adjusts the baseball cap she is wearing, which she had hoped would make it harder to be recognized. She looks right and left, wondering if running away is still an option, but his eyes are on her. She stays put.

"I knew you'd be here," she whispers.

Once he realizes it's truly her he stands up, arms wide open. She stalls. The air is fresh and clean and yet she finds it hard to breathe. He points to the bench.

"Want to sit down?" he asks, tears rolling down his withered cheeks.

She opens up her purse and pulls out a tissue packet. After handing it to him, she takes a seat, placing her purse as a barrier between them.

"You know my name is Paula."

He gives her a look like the one she once saw in a dog that had just been run over in the middle of a busy intersection. A dog she didn't stop to help because she was running late for an appointment that was important for her at the time. She has often felt guilty about leaving the dog there, alone. It has been years, yet Paula feels ashamed whenever she remembers. A dog she could have helped but didn't. That vivid image of a dog staggering about to collapse still gives her sleepless nights. Wondering if he, this man sitting on the bench beside her, has ever felt the same way. How such feelings play out when you're talking about human beings and not dogs. Does death by indifference – death by inaction – have a name, other than murder?

"Paula, yes," he says after a long silence. He can't stop staring at her while fidgeting with the tissues, turning one after another into a small ball between his hands. "You've not changed at all."

Oh, yes, I've changed. You've no idea how I've changed. But instead of saying so, Paula smiles at him without showing her teeth.

"Have you changed?" she replies.

"I never stopped looking for you, Adr... Paula. We never stopped looking for you, waiting. Hoping you'd call."

It's obvious to her that he hasn't changed. He has aged, of course, but remains good at dodging topics he doesn't want to touch. She wants to say she was never his to wait for, but a hummingbird sipping nectar from a beautiful orange flower distracts her. How many times has she heard people say that they wished they could fly away and leave everything behind. But one thing life has taught her is that you can never really leave. That wherever it is you fly to, you always drag your misery along. Human beings are made

3

up of 70 per cent water and 30 per cent of their past; what is done to them is indelible. This, Paula knows for sure.

"I was very far away. I couldn't—"

He doesn't let her finish her sentence.

"I understand, baby girl. No need to explain. What matters is you're here now! You have no idea how much I missed those blue eyes of yours."

He used to say her eyes matched the flag, and that she should be immensely proud of forever carrying her homeland within her. When she grew up, however, Paula couldn't bear to look at herself in the mirror, so she wore tinted contacts. She said they were a fashion statement and liked them because they matched her mood, her fate – and the horror of believing that her eyes embodied everything she had lost, or grown to hate.

"How's Ana María?" she asks, proving she can also dodge a subject that makes her feel uncomfortable. He frowns, and looks down at his shoes. They're clean and shiny, as usual. His Sunday shoes. He has probably been to Mass early that morning. She hasn't been to church, not since leaving the country. Another abyss she has to thank him for.

Instead of answering her question about Ana María, the man lifts his hand and tries to hold hers. Paula leaps up from the bench, as if stung.

"I'm sorry! I'm sorry!" he apologizes, looking mortified, gesturing clumsily.

"Don't touch me!" she hisses, her voice rising. A man walking his dog stops to look at her. The dog decides that it is a good place to defecate, and it does. The man walks away without cleaning up after his pet. She had spent the previous day walking around the city, stepping over dog turds left on the sidewalks, crossing paths with dog walkers who, like those in New York or Toronto, were holding multiple leashes. Here they were incapable of stooping to clean up, utterly oblivious to what they were doing to their own hometown. A perfect reflection of what this country is about. Too bad no one else has realized that the greatness of a nation can also be measured by how many of its people are actually willing to clean up their own shit.

"Please sit down again, baby girl. I'm sorry."

She takes a deep breath...and a seat on the bench once more, only this time a few inches farther away from him. He puts a tissue ball inside his pocket, and places the tissue packet close to her purse.

"Ana María died," he says, biting his lower lip. Paula takes in his words slowly; they hurt like stab wounds. She has been hoping to see Ana María. Hear her voice, smell her perfume. Anaïs Anaïs, all the rage while she was growing up. A few years ago, she found a small bottle of it at a discount store and bought it. She dabbed a little of it on her pillow and cried. Helpless; alone.

"How did she die?" she gathers the courage to ask.

He looks down at his shoes again as if that's the place where the right words to say can be found, lifts his gaze and fixes it on the river. A small boat is passing by. They hear laughter.

"You don't need to know. It doesn't matter."

"Yes, it does!" she replies, firmly. "I want to know."

He shakes his head, No.

"Tell me! I have a right to know!"

He pauses for a few seconds.

"She killed herself."

Paula puts her fist to her mouth and bites on her first knuckle. It's what she does when she doesn't want to scream. She can't say a single word. He seems to understand. He'd always known what she wanted to say before she said it.

"She just never got used to it," he says, matter-of-factly.

"Used to what?"

"To life without you."

Paula buries her face between her knees, hugs her legs tight, and cries. Loud, intermittent sobs, her shoulders shaking.

After a few minutes she lifts her head, wipes her face with her T-shirt, and when he offers her a tissue, slaps his hand as hard as she can, surprising herself. His hands used to seem big and strong. Now they're bony and blotchy with age spots. He pulls back, afraid of her.

"How dare you blame me?"

"I don't blame you. I'm just telling you the truth," he replies, rubbing his hand where she hit him. "She couldn't live without you. No: she didn't want to live without you. I did what I could to help her, but it was useless. We just missed you so much!"

She gets to her feet and walks away, toward the river. The water is calm and deep, brownish. Nature's perfect hiding spot. No wonder they used it to dump bodies. A colossal oxymoron, this strange beast in front of her: its water a peculiar womb that both embraces the dead while nourishing the hopes of the living. At least, those who still have hope and can feel proud.

"I wish you'd let me explain things to you," he says, getting up as well and approaching her at a safe distance. The park has been slowly filling with people, families out to have fun, playing. The way the man and Paula used to do in another life, once upon a time. "And you shouldn't leave your purse unattended back there on the bench. This is not Canada, you know? People steal a lot here."

"So you knew where I was," she says turning to look at him.

"Yes," he replies, blushing slightly.

"And you never came to look for me. Instead, you let Ana María kill herself."

He brings his hands to his head. It's obvious to her that he's unable to hide his desperation.

"Adriana, don't be so unfair. I couldn't just go looking for you! And I saved her twice before she finally succeeded."

Perverse how he attached success to suicide as if it were the most natural combination. Don't forget who you're dealing with. Why you came back.

"No, you couldn't just come looking for me, that's true. And my name is Paula!"

He lets out a sigh that sounds almost like a grunt.

"Please. Let me explain."

Paula waits a little, knowing every second of her silence hurts him. She wants to hurt him, and enjoys her small power, before relenting.

"I'm all ears," she says, adjusting the cap on her head, closing her eyes, lifting her face to the sun. Here, on the other end of the continent, the sun feels different – apologetic, perhaps. As if trying to make it up to her, to everyone for the chaotic state of affairs in the land.

The man walks back to the bench to fetch Paula's purse. He appears surprised at its weight, but he's sensible enough not to ask. He simply places it on the ground close to where they are standing now, and they both can see it. Then he tucks his hands into his pockets, and gazes into the horizon.

"They were shitty times, baby girl."

A boy runs past them, chasing a red ball. Laughing. Neither the man nor she manage to smile.

"We were at war."

"Tell me something I don't know. And stop calling me 'baby girl.'"

He nods abjectly.

"Well, we were at war and—"

"And whose side were you on, huh?" she interrupts.

The man takes his hands out of his pockets and cracks his knuckles, one by one. Paula cringes. She forgot this is what he does when he's nervous or upset.

"I love this country. I wanted it to be safe, a country in unity. And there were people doing everything they could to prevent that."

"People like my parents, you mean."

He chooses not to answer.

"They were putting bombs everywhere. Blowing up people's houses, buildings. Creating chaos. If you didn't shoot the hell out of them, they'd shoot the hell out of you. That's simply how it was."

"So that's why you and your friends had to burst into their houses, to kidnap, torture, and kill them, right? It was the patriotic thing to do." The man is shifting his weight from one leg to the other, clearly not knowing what to say or do. Paula looks at the river and remembers he doesn't know how to swim. She wonders if she could get away with pushing him into the water and letting him drown. Death by drowning is silent.

"I didn't kill anyone, I swear."

8

She finds it impossible to remain silent.

"You did – just by working with them."

Another boat goes by. People wave. Paula and the man don't respond and are booed for their lack of enthusiasm. Someone, in a shrill voice, probably a teenager, calls them a couple of lame asses.

"They always called me after the fact."

"What do you mean?" she asks, genuinely eager to know.

"To tell them if... To make sure they were dead."

A wave of rage takes over her body.

"I was so proud of you when I was little, saying you were a doctor." She pronounces the word doctor with contempt, to emphasize her disgust. "Turns out you were a doctor who helped to kill."

"No, I didn't! I just told them...if they were really dead."

Paula closes her fists, hits her hips. Hard. Hard enough for it to hurt.

"And if they were not really dead? What then? You stayed there until they had been tortured enough to die?"

She can tell he's irritated by her hitting herself, and gets ready to hit him instead if he comes anywhere near her.

"No! I brought them back to life. I saved them!"

"So they could be electrocuted some more? How kind of you," she retorts, letting out a bitter guffaw. The man takes a few seconds to respond. Paula can tell he's trying to find the right words.

"No, I never worked in those...centres."

This time she laughs out loud, without holding herself back.

"You're the king of euphemisms. Congratulations."

"Look!" he says, exasperated. "If it helps you to know this, your parents were never tortured. They died quickly, all right? In their own bed. And when I got there, they were already dead."

Paula can't keep herself together anymore. She lets out a scream. A long, intense scream. The man looks around, nervously. People are staring at them, alarmed.

"Why don't we go talk about this somewhere else?" he says.

She detects fear in his voice.

"No. I don't want to go anywhere with you. Last time I did, I lost my identity and my childhood." She's crying now, and hating herself for it.

"You didn't lose your childhood. We gave you a wonderful childhood. You were loved, and we took really good care of you."

"Yes. But you're forgetting a small detail: I was not yours."

He can't stay beside her. The weight of her words forces him to return to the bench. It's windy. He feels out of breath. His heart is pounding, his back covered in sweat.

"I'm old," he tells her from the bench. "I don't feel well."

A little girl who was blowing soap bubbles is not blowing bubbles anymore but standing still, staring at them. The girl's mother is keeping guard close to her child, probably wondering if she should intervene, or call the police. Paula picks up her purse from the ground and returns to the bench, trying to feign normalcy. The conversation is not over yet.

"Why did you take me?" she asks, wiping her eyes with the back of her hands, again placing her purse as a small wall between them.

"I earned you," he says quietly.

"You what?" She turns to face him completely, in disbelief.

"I thought I had earned you," he corrects himself, avoiding her eyes.

"You *earned* me?" Paula makes an enormous effort to remain calm.

"You have to understand. Ana María and I had waited for so long to have a child, so long! And then I heard you crying and there was no one there. Those bastards had done...what they did, and you were next door, in your room, eyes wide open, crying." His voice is breaking, but he goes on. "You, with those baby-blue eyes I immediately adored, all alone in that room. You were barely a year old. I panicked. I didn't know what to do, there was no one else, no one I could call, and I couldn't leave you alone there, with no one to care for you! I knew of others who had taken babies, or received babies, and I thought, why not us? Why not Ana María and me? We were good people, good citizens, and we were the best parents we could be for you. We loved you so much!"

"So I was your prize? For being loyal to a murderous regime?"

"I already told you I never killed anyone."

"The hell you didn't," she replies, clenching her teeth, forcing herself not to yell. "My father's mother died after he was killed. My aunt, my father's sister, was the one who found my parents dead at home. She killed herself after that, couldn't live with the memory. Can you blame her? It was too much for my grandmother to bear, losing both her children in less than a year. And I was nowhere to be found. She was a widow, she thought she had nothing to live for. I was told she died of sadness, and I believe it. Those deaths are on you. And my other grandmother, the one who took me with her to Canada... She was so scared of you, of your connections, and of your trying to get me back, that she couldn't stand staying in her homeland any longer. We were forced to escape. I was forced to grow up far away from here and never tell anyone my story. Who would believe it, anyway? But who am I kidding here. You'd never understand, obviously. You've never had to endure such sorrow."

"Ana María's sorrow doesn't count? And my own? We couldn't eat, we couldn't sleep after you were gone. Ana María used to lock herself in your room for days on end, sleeping in your bed, surrounding herself with your clothes, crying, screaming, and there was nothing I could do that would soothe her. We all suffered!"

Paula has finally had enough. She stands up, and gets ready to leave. She can't listen anymore.

"You suffered?" she says, grabbing her purse. "Did you ever stop to think that I lost my parents not once but twice? That you took me away from my family, and then they took me away from you, and away from here, and I ended up growing up never feeling like I belonged anywhere? Did you ever stop to think about what you had done to me?"

Paula takes off the baseball cap and shows him her balding scalp. Her head looks like an abandoned doll's. He's perplexed. Terrified, almost.

"What happened to your beautiful golden hair?" he demands to know, then immediately softens his tone. "Do you have cancer?"

Paula shakes her head.

"I've been pulling it out."

"Why?" he asks, making an effort to seem kind, but instead the tone of his voice sounds as if he were asking, "Are you crazy?"

"It's Trichotillomania. Another souvenir from my time with you."

The man's eyes well up again and he stretches his hand to touch her.

"My poor baby girl!" he says. "I'm so sorry! Please forgive me!"

She moves a couple of steps away from him, puts on the cap again, and slides one of her hands inside her purse.

"I have a gun" she says, quietly.

The man stares at her, not comprehending.

"I have a gun. If you say anything or you make any suspicious movement, I'll shoot you."

Paula's voice is suddenly deeper than before. The man's body stiffens.

"Take off your shoes," she says.

"But..."

"I said, take off your shoes."

The man does as he is told. His movements are slow. It's hard for him to untie the laces. His fingers are shaking.

"Now take off your socks."

The man complies while Paula looks around, making sure no one is watching. Without losing sight of him, Paula picks up the shiny shoes and socks and feeds them to the river.

"You'll have to dive in to get them, or walk barefoot all the way back home, where the police are probably waiting for you already. A file has been opened to investigate your role in the killing of my parents and my kidnapping. I'll testify against you, you bastard."

She turns and walks away. People around her are doing what families do on Sundays at the park: playing ball, picnicking, biking, jogging, some simply enjoying the sunshine, others deep into their phones. Everyone blissfully unaware of what she has been through. Who else here, she wonders, who else was complicit with the regime during those days? Who else is walking freely around the park after taking part in the atrocities committed when she was a child?

A woman is selling balloons. Paula buys them all and, as a present to her parents up above, releases them into the air. As she walks away, her shoulders relax. She stops, opens her purse, and takes out the small cobblestone brick, letting it fall into the long grass at the side of the path, relieved to be rid of the weight.

IN TRANSIT

Name: Eulalia. Middle name? Don't have one. When I was little they called me Lalita, but no one remembers that now. Last name: Martínez de Jesús. I wanta ask him how come he don't recognize me.

It's the fourth time they catch me, fourth time they ask me the same old questions. And in four times, this *güero* – this Blondie – has been in charge of me twice. We all look the same to him. But sure as shit I can tell them *gringos* apart 'cause I pay attention to who's having a hairy beard or who's got fuzz that almost don't cover his pink chin or if his teeth are crooked or so straight that he can smile like he loves life on TV. Almost none of them *güeros* have crooked teeth. But the other ones, the ones who are brown-skinned like us but pretend not to understand what we say, those have smiles like corn cobs: yellow, uneven.

I feel like asking Blondie here how come he don't realize it's the second time I'm taking a turn with him, for all this give-me-your-name shit. Haven't slept in such a long time... I refuse to fall asleep, so I talk to myself all the time. Don't know why people look at me funny. All I've got left to keep me from falling asleep is my own voice so I need to hold on to it because that other voice is just waiting for me to go quiet and close my eyes, waiting for me to let my guard down so it can come and tell me the same thing over and over again. It's got me full up to here with sadness and depression. I wanta tell my *güero* all about how I feel, and what's been going on, to see if he'll give me a chance. Can't. He's already busy with someone else.

There's a guy with a bandage 'round his head. Dark, red stains dried up on the cloth. He must've tried to run. There's a woman with a baby that won't stop crying. Who knows how long she's been on the move. We all walk across the border with nothing. You walk and walk and walk and keep walking till heat wrings you out like a rag. So you limp and crawl under the sun with no protection other than your will to get here. And then, this.

"People are stubborn, man! They just don't get it, do they?" one of them *güeros* says to my *güero*. And my *güero* nods big with his pink-and-yellow head. I wanta answer no, you don't get it, but it's no use. We're not the same. They smell fresh. Like laundry. We smell of skank and sweat. But we don't even talk the same.

Take Manuel - he makes everyone call him Don Manuel as a mark of respect, but even with all that land of his he don't speak good. He always says "people is." My father said that, too. And me also. Until my son Andrés corrected us, that sharp little kid! He didn't care that we was actually at Don Manuel's house eating the sheep Don Manuel himself had just killed to celebrate his fiftieth birthday. Don Manuel said, "People is happy today" and he, Andrés, sprung up out a nowhere like a scrawny grasshopper and corrected him to his face, "You don't say people *is*, you say people are. Teacher said so." What saved him was it being the teacher who'd said what he said, 'cause no one in town woulda messed with that. We was lucky 'cause Don Manuel was already a bit drunk, so he laughed instead. "Well, you learned something all right, kiddo! Too bad it's something useless." Don Manuel's gap in his front teeth looked like an open door.

Ever since I was caught I've been remembering things. At least in this room there's fans. Back home it's never been as hot - not even on the worst day. Here, night alone shows some compassion. The air cools down and right away you're grateful for the most generous permission you'd never heard of: permission to breathe.

Sometimes I'm sure what happened to my son is my fault. But if I think about it I cry, and if I cry then I get tired and wanta sleep. And I don't wanta sleep. Andrés was so stubborn! I wanted him to go to school. And he went. He went every day until I got hurt and I couldn't work anymore. I pretend I don't, but I do see when people stare at my hand. That's why it's strange my *güero* didn't remember me. I don't think many people show up here with a deformed hand like this, like mine. Of course, how can I judge? There's way too many who come here all beaten up, dehydrated, and exhausted. Perhaps there's many others that look even worse than me. God's generous. He gives everyone a cross of their own.

Andrés wasn't born for a life like ours, farming the fields. He was nothing like his father – may God rest his soul. My son loved books. He wanted to finish high school. Even go to college. He wanted us to move to the city. But how was we going to do that? Without no money, my hand all crooked, and he so small and skinny – we had no one except each other. Where was we going to go, exactly?

At night he spent hours on end going over his books. He looked at them words the way other boys look at girls' tits. He read them so much that I used to ask him to stop. I was afraid his eyes was going to wear out them words. Just around then Don Manuel's youngest, a boy named Pepe, came up with the idea of going north. Being smuggled across the border with a *pollero* and finding work there. My first reaction was no, no, and no. And I wouldn't give in to him. Pepe got us together – his brothers and his father and me and Andrés – and gave us "strong arguments" (that's how he said himself, "strong arguments") to defend his plan. Andrés was good with numbers. Pepe was good at farming. If they left together and helped each other they'd make it for sure. "And we'd live like *gringos*, Mah! Can you imagine?" Andrés said. But he didn't need to say nothing. The way his eyes was shining said it all.

To tell you the truth, thinking about it that way, yes, it sounds really nice. But I again said no. What was they thinking? Andrés had just turned sixteen, still too young to just leave. But it was hard to make him understand. Half of the men in our town was already gone. Andrés and Pepe thought it'd be easy to do the same. "If we don't make it on our first try, then on the second one for sure we'll not fail, Mah. Just imagine how great things are going to be!" And he almost made me dizzy talking about all the things we would do. What we would buy with them American dollars he was going to earn? It wasn't that I didn't wanta have a huge TV – anyone wants a huge TV, right? And everything else. But I still said no. He must wait until he was older. Oh, but he was stubborn! Wanted to leave right away.

For a few days we didn't talk about nothing. I hadn't seen him so sad ever since the day we buried his father. "And how we going to pay the *pollero* to take you across the border, son?" I asked him one morning. It was still dark outside. His eyes lit up and pointed at the exhausted land outside our window. That's why I say maybe what happened was my fault, 'cause I sent him to school and then I got hurt, and he had to take over the field, and just then came the drought. Everything piled up.

After days and days of bugging me, I finally said yes. I told him I'd had it. He could stop being so annoying. I'd sell my little patch of land so he could go. He jumped up and down with joy, hugged me, and promised he'd work very hard to earn back them American dollars. He promised he'd buy me a much better house. And because I had always wished for a cow, he even promised me a cow, even though with this hand of mine I wouldn't ever be able to milk her. Pepe, Andrés, and a nephew of Don Manuel's called El Bizco for his crossed eyes (but he was actually quite clever), decided to make the journey together.

I sold my land and my house but was allowed to stay there until Andrés made it to the other side. Then I would move somewhere else. I used to pray a lot back then. Ever since Andrés got in him this idea of leaving, all I did was pray. And on the morning they actually left, me and Don Manuel took the three boys all the way to the altar to give them our blessing. We gave them their backpacks stuffed with tortillas, chiles, apples and bottled water. Andrés took what little money I put together for him. I did everything the way I was supposed to. And after I saw the bus disappear I was worried sick. Don Manuel said that for the first time in his life he was glad his wife was dead, 'cause she woulda never let Pepe go. She woulda never been able to stand the fear and anguish that was piercing his stomach, he said. I cursed Andrés' father the entire day. If he wasn't dead, our life would've stayed the same, and he would've never left. And if someone had been forced to leave it would've been him, the father of Andrés, not my son. And that woulda been easier. Or less hard.

In the end Andrés, Pepe, and El Bizco managed to get across but they was caught by the Border Patrol. When they phoned Don Manuel they told him that *la migra* had sent them back. "Deported" was the word, I remember. Now I know what it means, and how much it stings. But back then I didn't really get it, except for the money I had paid and lost.

19

I remember them boys all frustrated and angry 'cause they walked a lot and they were about to reach the highway where they was going to be picked up. I wanted Andrés to return. I would find a way to buy back my place, and pretend this never happened. Andrés wouldn't hear of it. He said they knew the way now. They knew exactly where to turn around so that the same thing didn't happen again. And they was going to risk it one more time, the three of them alone. Just not to regret not giving it another try. Stubborn as a mule, like always.

Before hanging up he told me the heat was fierce. Those were his words exactly. That's how he said it: "Mah, the heat is fierce here." He didn't say anything about the rest: how they was chased down and beaten up when they got caught. El Bizco told me all about that later. I stare now at the guy sitting here with a bandage 'round his head and wonder if my Andrés looked like him. Or maybe even worse.

Less than a week later, the phone rang again. It was already getting dark and Don Manuel picked up right away. There we was, me and his other sons, huddled together waiting for news. As soon as we saw the expression on his face we knew something was very wrong.

"They failed," he said as he hung up. The only one who was okay was El Bizco. He'd been the one to call. They got lost in the desert. Pepe was in the hospital. They was going to send him back home once he was doing better.

"What about Andrés?"

After the Novena I quit praying. I wasn't afraid of God's punishments. What was He going to take away from me, anyways? I had lost my son, my house, my land. I had nothing. Don Manuel let me move into a tiny room where he kept odds and sods. I woulda stayed there had my son not come to talk to me. First I thought it was a dream. I was half asleep; it was dark. But then his voice grew stronger, saying, "Mah, I'm very thirsty, give me some water." I shut my eyes tight and covered my head with my blanket. No use. Then I sat up on my cot. His voice was still there. I ran out of the room and into the fields. I wanted to scream. It didn't matter where I went, I still could hear Andrés saying, "Mah, I'm very thirsty, give me some water." When my eyes are wide open like right now and there's people around, for example, I don't hear him. But if I stop talking and remain quiet, his voice reaches me clearly. And I can't find any calm. That's why I asked El Bizco to guide me to the exact same place where they tried to get across the second time. He refused. Thought I was going mad.

I wanta go where my *güero* is standing and ask him if I look mad to him. See what's his answer. Yes, my clothes are dirty and sticking to my skin 'cause of the dust and heat. And I'm tired. But I don't care. No. I'm not crazy. Everything hurts. My legs hurt, my back hurts. Breathing hurts. My friends didn't believe me. They said I was imagining things. Wanted to take me to church. To church? What for?

That's why I had to do it on my own. May Don Manuel forgive me for taking his watch and the money in his wallet. Oh, well! Nothing to do about that now.

So that's why I'm sitting here in this godawful detention centre surrounded by sand and shrubs. During the day the sun lashes at you with no mercy. I'm never sure in which direction I got to walk. Every single time I try to go across the border I get caught. They ask my name, lock me up in this room with others as desperate as me, and then send me back. They don't let me explain anything.

I don't wanta stay in their country. I see who smiles at us; who lets it show that we disgust them. Who doesn't even want to look us in the eye. I see them – their teeth and beards and chins, hoping they'll see me, too. Hoping they'll listen. I stare at my *güero* again. Wanta beg him. But he don't even look at me. All I've got left's my own voice. And my boy's tireless whispers. Before they lead us out and push us in the van I give my *güero* one last look. He don't turn around. His hair's messy. The shirt of his uniform is wrinkled. I hope they won't catch me again. I hope I don't hafta come here ever again. But just in case, I try to take everything in: the naked light bulbs, the bare, worn out walls, the smell of dry blood, sweat, and piss.

The woman with the baby lines up ahead of me. So does the guy with the bandaged head. The baby is not crying no more. My *güero*'s back is still turned to us. I wish I could explain to him that all I wanta do is bring my boy some water.

Water for my boy, *güero*, you see? That's all I'm here for. To bring him water to calm his thirst.

DECALOGUE
FOR A DOLL
WITHOUT A HOUSE

Facts: once upon a time there was a woman who decided she couldn't be a mother anymore, so she went away and never came back. She left behind a broken home with broken children, and a doll that survived up until another unforgiving December night. Synopsis: a broken woman left behind a broken girl who became a woman with a broken doll. But that's not the end. It's the beginning. It was, at least, for me. And you, my niece, the only other female in this family, you need to know our side of the story so that one day you'll be able to shape your own.

A few days after we got engaged, Albert and I were going back to Father's house after visiting some of his friends. I had no friends of my own except for Isabella, but I had already stopped seeing her, so when we went out it was always to visit friends or colleagues of his. We found an organ grinder on the street who had a monkey standing on the instrument collecting coins from passersby with a hat. The monkey was wearing a pink jacket. It was cold, and I felt sorry for him. Norway is no country for monkeys. He was shivering. His eyes were sad, vacant almost, yet the tune he was playing was happy. The tarantella Mother danced for Father at our neighbours' house the last Christmas we were together. I was little but I remember how graceful she was, how she smiled as she moved her hands and feet to the rhythm. The music was a stiletto in my stomach, it left me almost breathless. You will learn, as you grow older, that your body, your skin has a memory of its own. That memory is merciless.

I needed to escape the music.

"I'm not feeling well, can we go, please?"

"Don't be silly, you were fine a second ago!" Albert replied, not even looking at me. He was making faces at the monkey who, in turn, wasn't paying attention to him.

"Let's keep on walking, can we?"

"Why walk when we can dance?" he said, taking me by the hand, bowing playfully, still trying to catch the monkey's attention.

I didn't want to dance. I was afraid I might throw up, so I pulled my hand away and turned my back against him in order to cover my mouth. He grabbed my arm so hard it hurt. When I raised my eyes I discovered that once again he was not looking at me. Not at the monkey, either. He was looking all around us, seeming to say, *Did you see her reject me?* Smiling through clenched teeth.

"Don't you ever humiliate me in public," he hissed, his mouth close to my ear, tobacco and whisky on his breath. It was a smell I usually liked, but not then. I tried to get him to loosen his grip on my arm, but his fingers sank deeper into my skin.

"You're hurting me!" I complained in a low voice, trying not to attract anyone's attention. That made him angrier. Two very well-dressed gentlemen walked past us, and gave a coin to the monkey. Then kept walking.

"Not more than you just hurt me," he answered and dragged me away, never letting go of my arm until we arrived at Father's house. I was trying hard not to cry because I sensed tears would make things worse. I wanted to explain to him how the music had made me feel, and why, but there was no chance. He didn't let me talk.

24

"Now, you must think about your behaviour today, my dear, and promise to be better in the future." He blew me a kiss before I closed the front door.

When I came in, Father and Anne Marie asked me how I was. I told them everything was fine and rushed to my bedroom. Albert had left a bruise on my arm, yet the pain I felt was beyond skin-deep. The next day, Albert pretended nothing had happened. But I never forgot that chilly afternoon, and that monkey's sadness. And I remembered the tarantella, its notes twirling in my mind – as if knitting a rope around my neck.

Too late, I realized that the monkey was an omen I should've heeded.

Truth number one: Omens can present themselves in a shape you least expect.

Stained by my Mother. That's how I felt growing up. People said horrible things about her, horrible things Anne Marie denied and told me to disregard. I knew she was right, because in my mind Mother remained sweet and caring, not the heartless being she was made out to be after she'd left. Yet, I always felt that people looked at me and thought, *Her mother was a monster who abandoned her poor husband.* I wondered if my brothers, Ivar and Bobby – your dad and uncle – felt the same, but I never summoned the courage to ask them. Men know how to manage. Take Father: after Mother left, he became a special kind of victim. A hero, almost, because he was raising his children on his own. Not on his own, of course, but who would ever acknowledge Anne Marie? She was a nanny; paid help. Never mind that she was paid very little. Never mind that after

Mother left there was no more music in our house, no more dancing; there were no more hidden chocolates and macaroons to be had as treats when Father wasn't looking. I missed music the most, but I felt like crying when I thought about it. Then, time and silence eroded the memory. Or so I had believed.

Mother's absence felt like a scar, and for years I thought it was there, across my face for everyone to despise. I was sure that everywhere I went people knew I had not been wanted enough, not loved enough, even though I had a beautiful doll whose mere existence seemed to contradict that feeling. Anne Marie told me that Father didn't have much money back then. Mother had to work, too, to make ends meet. But the doll must have cost a little fortune and Mother still bought her for me, with a small cradle. Anne Marie told me that Mother was sure I'd "rip it to ribbons." Those were Mother's words, "rip it to ribbons." What she was thinking when she paid for the doll? Father liked to say, "The way she spent money, it burned her hands." He thought people who were careless with money were weak – and weak meant inferior. But now I know that Mother was actually the strongest of us all, because she broke free.

Truth number two: You have to be ready to look beyond the surface to discover what is evident but no one else wants to see.

Girls didn't want to be my friends. They were afraid their mothers might leave them, too, as if leaving your family were a contagious disease. I spent most of my years at school all alone, in class and in the school's courtyard. Until Isabella arrived. Long black hair, olive skin; an outcast, too. We understood we had only each other and quietly held hands, shared our secrets. But I don't think we ever shared our pain. That came later.

My brothers got involved in brawls and fights but Father, instead of scolding them, encouraged them to "Man up!" and show their peers who was the strongest. That was how Ivar's nose got forever crooked and how your uncle Bobby lost his front teeth – although he didn't tell the real story to your aunt and I was forbidden to mention it. She probably still believes his golden teeth are a souvenir from his brief stint in the army.

Then Father introduced me to Albert, and he seemed to make me forget that pain. I was young, about to finish school, unsure about what to do with my life. I wanted a job, but Father frowned on the idea. Back then, women were not supposed to work outside their home. Would I be forced to remain in Father's house forever, watching life go by? The thought scared me. Albert found me at a most vulnerable moment, and from the beginning I sensed that Father wanted him to rescue me, offer me a new, more comfortable life.

"Good morning, Miss Emmy," he would greet me. "I brought you flowers so they could see what real beauty looks like."

Isabella and I laughed at his compliments when we were alone, but when she told me to be careful, I couldn't help but think she was probably a little jealous. Meanwhile, Albert's smile and his perseverance slowly gained my trust. I felt safe and, for the first time, even strong. My Father began to shrink in my eye; Isabella, too. She wasn't funny enough anymore; she wasn't interesting enough anymore. Her round face, her plump figure, her dark hair became all too familiar.

"What's going on with you? With *us*?" she asked one afternoon. I didn't know how to reply. I didn't know how to explain that I felt like

I had outgrown her, outgrown the apartment where I had spent my entire life surrounded by Mother's knick-knacks. I even felt like I had outgrown my family. I wondered if that was how Mother had felt?

When Albert proposed to me I considered myself the luckiest girl in the world.

"*Jeg elsker deg*," he whispered softly in my ear, and all of a sudden norsk had never sounded sweeter. I believed him when he said he loved me, and thought I could learn to love him, too. I was certain I would never need anyone else. I was ready to be his wife, and bring my doll to our house so that when we had a baby daughter it could be hers. And she would know, because I would tell her, that this doll was the last present I had been given by her grandmother. We would play together.

Truth number three: Always distrust the things you like. They are a trap.

Soon it would be Christmas and Christmas had never been a merry time at home, really, though we were good at pretending. The celebration never again was as extravagant as it had been the last Christmas that Mother spent with us, when she got Ivar some new clothes and a sword, a trumpet and a horse for Bobby, and the doll and cradle for me. But the coming Christmas would be my first as a newlywed; my new life would begin. Albert convinced me that the perfect date for us to marry would be a day in mid-December: it would give me a reason to be cheerful in spite of the grey weather, the cold wind, the upcoming anniversary of Mother's departure, and people's insufferable seasonal joy.

After our engagement, Anne Marie was allowed to leave me alone with Albert in the sitting room whenever he came to visit, and he took those opportunities to hold me closer to him and begin teaching me about love. He was gentle at first. I enjoyed the taste of cigar in his mouth, the warm moist of his tongue. I couldn't help but sigh and feel excited when it circled my ears. We were careful and quiet. He would put his hand on my dress and gently caress my breasts while we kissed, and although at first I rejected his advances, trying to behave modestly, as I knew Anne Marie and Father expected me to, I found it hard to stop him once he had begun. Albert was the kind of man who would not take no for an answer, so I had to come up with little games and excuses to get him off me. "Wait until you're my husband," I would say, smiling, acting like a teacher scolding a small child, to which he would always reply with an animal roar, and we laughed.

When the time came to choose a place to live, he bought it without telling me about it first. When I tried to protest, he was upset.

"But Emmy! How can you not be pleased? It's a beautiful apartment, very modern and full of light, wait until you see it!"

I did love it. As I loved the curtains and the furniture he chose. Anne Marie's only word of advice: "Do not go against your future husband's wishes if you want to have a happy marriage." I wanted a happy marriage so much that I pretended to love burgundy napkins I abhorred, the boring but apparently pricey eighteenth century painting with which Albert decorated our future dining-room, the golden cross with ivory incrustations he hung over what was to be our bed. I accepted it all gracefully, and counted my blessings.

I wanted to tell Isabella all about these things, and how I truly felt; I began to miss her, but how could I go back to her after abandoning our friendship? I wanted her to be my bridesmaid, but Albert picked his cousin, and I did not feel ready to have an argument. It was going to be a lovely wedding. We would be happy, as we were supposed to be, and that was that.

Truth number four: Never expect life to turn out a certain way. You'll be disappointed.

The night before the wedding, everything changed. I was sitting by my bedroom window watching darkness enshroud the street. I set my gaze on silhouettes scurrying outside. They were probably trying to get out of the cold. I put my hand against the windowpane. It made me shiver. The temperature was surely going to fall even more; maybe it would snow. I dreaded snow. I dreaded everything white, especially that slab of laced ice, that trap hanging from my wardrobe's door: my wedding dress.

Albert had had it made especially for me with lace brought all the way from Brussels. I complained about the cost, no need to invest so much money on something that was to be worn only once.

"My bride will only own the best," he said. Father beamed when he heard Albert talk like that.

Father was frail: he couldn't be expected to take care of me much longer. His job at the bank had consumed him; his old respiratory illness had returned. When I heard him cough, when I saw him walk with difficulty to the coat rack to reach for his coat and hat before leaving for the bank every morning, I knew that he was only waiting for me to marry so that he could retire and live at peace.

Mother never came back, never sent any letters. Ivar and Bobby did not like to talk about her. They pretended they didn't remember how she used to play hide-and-seek with us, how she made funny voices and faces when reading us stories, how she loved dancing while she held us in her arms. I knew Anne Marie resented them for this. She had raised Mother, after all, and then she had raised us, but she had raised us because she had loved her so much in the first place. I haven't forgotten the many nights I heard her weep as she dusted Mother's belongings and turned our flat into a museum to her memory, a museum where her name was never spoken. After all her dedication to us, and to me in particular, dear old Anne Marie was surely relieved to finally see me off.

That is the reason why I simply could not find the strength to tell them what had happened to me that morning, while Father was still in the office and Anne Marie in the kitchen.

Albert came to visit me, like every day. He went to the sitting room with me, closed the door behind us, and hugged me. He started kissing the back of my neck, holding my waist with his hands. I dropped back my head and let him continue, trying to enjoy his embrace, thinking of what amusing excuse I would use to stop him, the day before our wedding. All of a sudden, he began to lift my dress. He had never done that before, never attempted to go so far. I froze. He turned me around so I would face him, and slipped his hand between my legs, pressing hard. I pushed him away.

"Don't touch me like that," I whispered so as not to alert Anne Marie while I tried to fix my dress.

He looked at me as if I was being unreasonable, sniffed his fingers and smiled.

"Surely you can't resent my wanting to have a little taste of what will be mine tomorrow."

I wanted to scream, slap his face.

"Tomorrow," he said, "there will be no more *no's.*"

Then he gave me a quick kiss on the cheek, brushed his hand against my breasts, and made his way out. Why had Albert suddenly behaved like that? I couldn't understand it, and was so upset that I went to my room to wash my face, my hands, and my neck before Anne Marie had a chance to see me. I wanted to wash him off my entire body. I could still feel his grip between my legs. I should have run to Isabella and asked her for help, but instead I threw up and, when Father came home in the afternoon, I acted as if nothing had happened.

"It's normal to feel nervous the night before the wedding," Anne Marie said that evening when she came into my room. Mother had been nervous as well, she told me. Mother had thrown up, too.

"Oh, my dear Emmy, you will be such a beautiful bride!" she exclaimed with a sigh as she fidgeted with the blinding-white crinoline before saying good night and leaving my room.

To calm myself down, I took the wedding dress and held it in my arms for a few moments. Then, for some reason I could not explain, I brought it to the window. I opened the glass pane and tossed it outside, on the empty road. I watched it fall like a gigantic, clumsy snowflake. The wind was blowing and I closed the window again so no sound would come in. Right away I knew I had to be quick, leave without looking back; I'd send letters later. I looked out the window and saw the fabric of my dress moving in the wind like the feathers of a dead bird.

All right, I didn't do that. But I wanted to. I did spend the entire night awake, sitting by the window, wondering if I should leave. It was the thought of Father that made me stay. I could not do to him the same thing Mother had done. I had to stay.

Truth number five: Acting against your instinct can be the single greatest regret in your life.

The following morning I couldn't even drink tea. I put on the white, expensive dress, and Father walked me to the altar. Albert's cousin was my bridesmaid. Nothing was the way I had dreamed of when I was a little girl.

It was a cold December day. The sky was blue and the sun shone but gave off no warmth. I had secretly wished for there to be a storm, or at least for it to be cloudy. The palms of my hands were clammy and my knees were shaking. After Albert had said "I will," it was my turn.

"Will you have this man to be your husband, and to serve him and keep him in sickness and in health?" the priest asked. I stayed silent, wishing I could answer no. I could hear Father cough behind me, sitting in the front pew, and Albert cleared his throat loudly, but without turning to look at me. I understood that those seconds, those mere seconds that I had needed to compose myself, nod and then whisper "I will," had probably been enough to make him feel humiliated and, therefore, furious.

After our wedding reception was over, I went with my husband to the fancy apartment he had bought for us. The honeymoon had to be delayed because Albert was busy closing some deals that were very important for his business, and he was required to stay in Oslo. Or so he said. It took me almost a year to realize he never had any intention of going on a honeymoon.

As my most precious possession, I brought along in my suitcase, in its own box, the doll that Mother had given me. Her blue dress had slightly faded, and her blond hair was unkempt. I hadn't paid attention to her for years, that was true, but I was still hurt by what Albert said.

"What do you have in there?" he asked with a mix of curiosity and disdain.

"A doll," I replied.

He let out a guffaw. "A doll? At your age? Ridiculous!"

I did not answer. I found a place for the box with my doll at the very back of the wardrobe that Albert had assigned to me. I sat down on our bed to await my fate.

He came close to me and lifted my wedding gown violently, forced me on my back, tore my underwear, and let out a scream of joy when he pushed himself inside me and confirmed I was, indeed, a virgin.

"Good girl!" he panted. His breath was no longer appealing to me, the smell of his sweat made me nauseous, but I knew better than to let it show.

Truth number six: You don't know what you're capable of doing, until you're forced to do it. That's how you learn how strong you are.

After that day, he would come home after work and force himself on me with such strength that sometimes I found it hard to sit down afterwards. How I yearned to go back to Father's house and beg for help, but it was impossible. I was so confused and embarrassed. Were all marriages like this? Was Albert's behaviour normal? In front of other people he was sweet and doting, but when we were alone he became a different person. Anne Marie and Father couldn't have handled hearing what my life was like. And I couldn't count on my brothers. They would just think I was as useless and

34

irresponsible as Mother, and that if I was unhappy I had only myself to blame. Of course, he didn't allow me to find a job. He wanted me to stay home and keep everything impeccable, to keep myself pretty for him – no more chocolates or macaroons, lest I gained weight. I remembered Mother eating treats when she thought no one could see her, and wondered if Father had been the same kind of man behind closed doors.

Then the unimaginable happened: I was late. That is when I finally broke down and went back to look for Isabella.

"Forgive me, I need your help. I can't be a mother. What if it's a girl? I can't pass on this curse."

Isabella listened to me, held my hands, caressed my hair, and found me help. Herbs. And she suggested I throw myself down a flight of stairs, protecting my head but trying to get my stomach hit. I did not tell Albert I was in touch with my only friend again. Then, the blessed hemorrhage came. *I'm going to hell for this*, I thought, but that was not true. I was already there.

Truth number seven: You don't go to hell. Hell comes to you.

Once the doctor left, Albert walked into our room, took a look at me – my eyes were so swollen that I could hardly see him – and declared:

"Don't worry, you'll recover soon. And you will give me a son."

Did he know what I had done? Was he suspicious? I didn't want to know, and was not going to ask. In the next few days, while Albert was not home, Isabella came to visit me once. Albert had hired a maid to take care of me and instructed her to never leave me alone, so it was not easy to find a moment to see Isabella, to thank her, to collapse in her embrace. I had to pretend I had a migraine. I sent the maid to a pharmacy on the other side of the city so I could have some time on my own. Isabella lay down beside me, braided and unbraided my hair as she reminded me of stories from our childhood; stories that I had long forgotten and she thought would lift my spirits. We remembered our school, our teachers, the poems we were forced to recite, the shoes we used to wear. Then she asked where my doll was. She remembered! So I got up and took my doll out of the box, and we both admired her and took turns holding her.

"She's so beautiful!" Isabella said, and I knew she meant it, but I could not feel any joy. I had already decided no baby of mine would ever hold that doll. She and I were condemned to be alone.

I was still holding my doll when Albert arrived back home.

Truth number eight: Nothing hurts more than a mother's empty arms.

Broken glass, broken mirror, broken doll, broken window. It would soon be Christmas again, and our first wedding anniversary, and I had just recovered from another "bleeding." The wind blew strong and icy and its power inspired me to act. *I will not be your organ grinder's monkey again, Albert. I'm going to leave you.* But he wouldn't let me. He threw his wineglass against the mirror and broke it. Aiming at me, he threw a vase but hit the window instead. He ran after me and made my jaw blue and swollen, and punched me until my ribs ached. When I was finally able to stand up, I discovered my doll's porcelain head had been smashed. There are no words to describe how I felt – how I feel even today, remembering it.

I knew that, in order to be able to leave, I would have to get Albert to calm down. So I forced myself to apologize to him, and promised I'd stay. I begged for forgiveness. To show I meant to be better, I began picking up the pieces of the broken mirror that were scattered on the floor.

"You know why I married you?" Albert asked, his voice as piercing as the glass pieces I was putting together in a pile. "To show the entire country that I could domesticate *you*, the daughter of the whore who ran away."

When he turned his back against me in order to leave the room, I knew it was my chance. I took the largest piece of the broken mirror and held it firmly in my hand, knowing it would cut us both, but hoping it would hurt him more.

Truth number nine: Blood bonds are sacred, and profaning the sacred can never be forgiven.

They say you always return to the places where you loved your life. I had never been in Italy before, but my arrival did feel like a return. This is the place where Father regained his health before I was born. The place where he and Mother spent their happiest months together. I wanted to see its beauty for myself. See the place where the sun is an actual star that caresses your skin.

I'm sorry I left behind such a huge stigma for you to carry. I had to escape, I couldn't risk being sent to jail and hurt our family even further. What was written about Mother in the papers back in the day, and what they said about me when it was my turn, was bad enough. I hope Father, Anne Marie, Ivar and Bobby found it in themselves to forgive me. And I hope you will do so, too.

I decided to write this letter hoping you will not tolerate the same humiliations that I grew up enduring. That you will not let any man choose your life. That you will be curious about the world out there, beyond the peace of home and the small circle of people who surround you.

To this day I still do not know where Mother went after she left us, but I'm sure she did well. As for me, I'm fine, too. I left home with only one suitcase that I packed in a hurry, and the box that held the pieces of my broken doll. I wanted to repair it but, in the end, chose not to. She's a reminder of what was and must never be again.

Truth number ten: To find true happiness, you must first face who you really are, and honour where you come from. My name is Emma Helmer, and my mother's name was Nora. A brave woman of whom you, too, should be proud.

PLAZA REQUIEM

I mix among the people who are protesting in groups, showing photographs, big signs with messages I don't dare read. Some are singing; others, sobbing. A group at the back chants for justice, fists up in the air. I try to look away but can't. I recognize two of the faces on large black-and-white posters. I feel a pang of anxiety. The images are old, and I've seen them many times. When I was little they were a source of pride. There's another face I can identify now – Elena's. Her story was unknown to me until recently. An urge to run away overtakes me, what am I doing here? I clench my teeth and force myself to keep walking: I'm here because I chose to be, because I need to see the plaza for myself. My hands are sweating, my knees shake. I'm glad – if I can be glad about anything – to have hidden my face behind dark glasses, to have my hair nested underneath this old baseball cap, to not have anything that might identify me. It is reassuring that nobody looks at me twice, because I couldn't hold anyone's gaze right now. Shame would break my face into pieces. I'm scared about what they might do to me. But I'm more scared about what has been done to them.

It's another anniversary and the square is filling up with memories. No one must find out how different mine are. I came because I wanted to join their protests – join them in their effort to never forget, although nothing that rests in my memory resembles what happened in this place.

Tanks had blocked the roads behind the Ministry of Foreign Affairs and the public housing building that's still there to the left.

There were many tanks coming so close side-by-side, that there was no way to escape. Sharpshooters were stationed on the roofs of the surrounding buildings. More tanks had come down from the main avenue.

As I walk around the edges, away from most of the people gathered here, I'm struck by an acid, aged smell. It must to be easy to lose control over your body when fear invades you with the certainty of a violent death. I wonder how much urine was mixed up with the blood of the dead... I don't dare ask those who were here and lived to tell about it – to describe, to confirm what we all know now... those bullets, the deafening explosions, the screams and cries that carve a tattoo inside your ears so deep that you can never sleep well again. I close my eyes very tight, tight, tighter, until it hurts. Then I shake my head like a dog shakes off water, trying to rid myself of what I've read, what I've heard. What no one ever told me.

Tanks and soldiers surrounded them, not leaving a space free for anyone to even breathe. They were as old as I am now. Students, like me. But they knew much more about life, because I've never been hungry, I've never feared jail, and nobody has ever snatched my loved ones from me to torture them, and then, to disappear them... I don't dare ask what is worse: to be certain that someone died here, in this plaza, in what might have been a more or less *quick* way (could it ever be quick enough?), or to be forever in the dark about what happened between the walls of a clandestine jail... What could be worse than to ask yourself how many hours did suffering have to be endured; to never know the whereabouts of that beloved person whose absence you came to cry about in this plaza today; to never know where the body finally turned to rot?

My homeland looks so different now... I haven't walked through its streets for such a long time. I wonder what he will say when he finds out I came? What will I tell him when we're together again? *Look, I just had to go to la Plaza...* Still, I shouldn't worry about explanations. I should worry about asking for them, but I know I'll never be brave enough.

My knees feel like they'll fail me. I'm afraid the slightest breeze might make me lose my balance. I nail my eyes to the asphalt that drowned in blood that day: it must have been very hard to try and run through scarlet puddles. I read once that blood smells like rusty metal. Bullets are made of metal. The blending must have been unbearable. How many shoes went missing in the rush; futile, trying to escape an inescapable army. The smoke made their eyes burn, they say. Doctors and ambulances were denied access, and so many of the wounded died waiting for help, as the dead lay beside them, eyes open. Soldiers piled them up, ordered to bury the corpses without counting them, without identifying anyone. How many mothers and sisters and fathers and brothers held their hopes high, expecting to find out that their loved ones were only missing, not really dead? They speak of thousands of missing persons during those years – over three hundred in this plaza alone. I close my eyes and try to imagine three hundred young people like myself running to escape the bullets, stomping each other, clawing at the floor and the walls... What was done to Elena I don't want to think about. It's enough that I remember the knife. I force myself to stay strong even though I know I'm approaching the exact spot where it happened. The biggest, brightest altar is set there.

I try to see the plaza in its silence, after everything was ended. I try to imagine what it feels like to see your friends die beside you, to bleed to death. I don't ask – I *can't* ask. I'm walking through sorrow: I feel it caressing my skin, oozing out of my people's pores.

Mother died before I could miss the feel of her skin. I'd always thought I would never need her, but now, in this place, I stand very still as I finally understand that you can never become used to such absences. My difference is, I know where her body is, I know she died peacefully. Morphine helped ease her pain. I suddenly understand what a privilege both her death and her grave are.

I turned seven years old the day this historic plaza became a killing field. I remember that afternoon very clearly. They were both there, Papa and my godfather, who I always called *Padrino*. He had strong, long arms. I loved how he threw me up in the air, and how he never missed my birthdays, no matter how busy he was. That same afternoon he gave me a magic set, and we started playing right away. Papa put a light bulb against his ear and it lit up, but only against his ear, not against mine, and I couldn't stop laughing. From between his fingers came coins that disappeared before my eyes, and from his suit he brought out long scarves knotted into an endless, colourful snake he put around my neck, calling me his *rainbow princess*... From a hat he took out Susa, so fragile and small.

"My own puppy!" I shrieked with joy, and Father and *Padrino* laughed. Their plan had worked. I'd never suspected my greatest wish was about to come true. It was the most magical, unforgettable afternoon ever. And the worst afternoon for the woman who is walking past me and who, in a broken voice that seeps through my skin and makes me feel unspeakably guilty, is praying loudly for her son.

I hadn't seen Papa give the order. I only remember *Padrino* leaving in a rush after patting my puppy's head and giving me a quick

kiss on the forehead. Everything must've happened without warning. I was holding Susa, busy choosing a proper name for her...
Papa refuses to speak about that day, and why he refused to let me
see my *Padrino* afterwards. He acts as if nothing ever happened, as
if breathing in another language is normal for us.

For a long time I didn't know the real reason why we had never
returned to our homeland, why he kept insisting that it didn't matter where we lived, or how we were called, as long as we stayed
together. So we had settled down in our modest Canadian home in
our rural Canadian town, without any guards or servants, just the
two of us, playing with the snow in winter. He said snow made
everything look clean, so soft and trouble-free. He said he felt at
peace with the world. I believed him, and never asked about the
past, though for many years I secretly wished for *Padrino's* return. I
missed his sense of humour, his strong arms holding me and tossing
me in the air.

It was hard for me to believe the newspapers, the reports; those
magazines I accidentally found online. They *had* to be mistaken.
Every day I thought, *Today will be the day I confront him*. And
every day, after watching him prepare dinner, having him help me
with my homework, and tend to old Susa with great tenderness, I
couldn't. I had decided back then to wait until I could return to the
plaza by myself.

I was shaking last night when I arrived at the airport. *Yes, I'm
here on holiday*, I told the immigration officer, my spoken Spanish
strange and rusty. Corroded. I didn't get much sleep in the hotel. So
many memories had come rushing back: my home-schooled years,
the palatial house where I'd spent my early childhood. Idle hours of
childhood calm, a stillness close to serenity. But I am finally here,

43

and I can't control my body, can't stop it shaking. I don't know how I'll look at my father's hands again, when I go back to him. I examine my own hands. Our fingers are the same. Long, slender. Even delicate. We'll never be able to escape who we are.

The altar is located against the wall of the church. It's a few metres wide, and looks taller than I am. There are dozens of candles, flowers, photos of people, pictures of saints. Incense permeates the air. Suffocating. It's hot and sunny, my shirt is soaked in sweat. Elena was a year younger than I am, seven months pregnant. She had tried to escape and had been arrested. I've seen photos of young people lined up against the wall, their pants pulled down, heads bleeding. Elena was among them but she was not tame, she had not followed orders like everyone else. Angry, she had yelled at the soldiers, insulting them. They say that's the reason why *Padrino* made an example of her. With his favourite knife. The silver one he always carried in a leather sheath that hung from his belt. The one he'd never allow me to touch because it was honed so sharp.

When I first read about it I found it impossible to believe. Witnesses said they'd seen him cut her belly open and tear the baby out. Nail him to the wall, I cried to myself. To *this* wall right in front of me. With his knife. The knife he wouldn't let me touch, because it was so sharp.

"You want trouble, *hijos de su reputísima madre?*" they say he yelled. I can imagine – no, *I can hear* him articulate each word. He was a man of precision. His hands always manicured. I wonder if *Padrino* had told Papa how it had happened, what he had done. I wish that I might find the strength to ask him one day if he'd felt proud of himself that afternoon, or horrified as I am now.

44

The scar on the wall makes me believe it all really happened. I believe it, and the brutality of it swamps me like a wave. There's no way out, no way back, no air. I fall to my knees – I can't breathe. A woman bends down.

"Do you need help, *mija?*"

Strange sounds I've never heard before are coming out of my mouth. A kind of burbling. A perverse gift of tongues. I want to scream. I try to pull myself together but when I feel the woman's soft embrace I break down. I'm broken.

"Call the paramedics! This girl here needs help!"

I shake my head furiously and push the woman away. I can barely see through my weeping, can barely stand up but I start walking away as fast as I can. I wish I had been able to pray for Elena and her baby, for those who had died under a regime headed by the person I love the most. I wanted to pray for them, for him, for myself, for us all. On my way out I bump into a person carrying a big sign: cannot avoid a photo of the most important men in my life, preening in their military uniforms. Serious, disciplined, young – just as I remember them. It's hard to believe a photo can say so much, and yet so little, about someone.

When I finally leave the plaza I look around to make sure nobody has followed me, no one has recognized me and, like never before, the weight of all that I lost that day falls on me. *You took away our homeland from us, Papá,* I think to myself, knowing that I'll never be able to say this to his face. *You stripped me of my city, my people, my language, my name. You bled us all.* I take my shoes off I don't know why. I simply feel the urge to touch this dry pavement – absorb its uneven, rough, warm surface – faintly drunk from the rays of the sun, exhausted by pain and more pain. I feel guilty for having pushed that gentle woman away. I should've thanked her, should've apologized. I wish I could've told her how truly sorry I am for her grief. But I'll never be able to because, while someone she loved died here on that infamous day – my birthday – my father was making magic for me. And there's nothing I can ever do to change that.

Barefoot, I keep on walking, hiding my face. People are still arriving. It seems to me the whole country has come together and my heart is pounding so hard I fear it will announce my presence: *Look at her! There escapes the daughter of the murderer you hate so much!* I'd like to hate him, too, only I can't. Even if he took away this land from me, even though it will never be mine again, I just can't. *Forgive me*, I murmur. I look at some children who are getting off a bus: in the way they hug their hurting parents or siblings, in the way they carry old family photos for everyone to see, in the way they hold their candles, ready to light them and march with their heads high, I know they already understand the importance of never forgetting. *Forgive him*, and I bite my lips so hard that I can taste my blood. It's only fair that I take this bitter taste with me. I'm taking the dust of my streets with me, too, on the soles of my bare feet. I want to touch what was once mine but it isn't anymore. As I board the bus to the hotel, a new certainty slips like a stiletto between my ribs. I, too, will never forget.

MARÍA TIMES SEVEN

Across the entire region, people spoke of Doña Toña's multiple births. Seven strong and healthy baby girls had issued from their mother's swollen belly, screaming at the top of their lungs. As soon as Doña Toña had finished breastfeeding the lot, a ravenous appetite roared again from those who'd been first to take their turns. For thirty days and thirty nights she didn't sleep, dutifully offering each child a nipple. After only a week of toil, each breast resembled the udder of a large cow. At the beginning, Doña Toña didn't have time to dwell on the changes her body was undergoing. It was only later, when others told her that she was growing smaller as the little girls were growing bigger – as if the milk her daughters drank robbed her of her self every day – that she decided to wean them. Choosing names for them was almost as difficult as distinguishing one from the other, so Doña Toña finally opted to call them all "María." That way she would never make a mistake whenever she called their names.

Doña Toña, the widow of a recently dead, wealthy landowner, and her seven Marías, lived in a large house on the outskirts of town. The girls often raised a deafening ruckus, because whatever befell one afflicted all with equal intensity. If one slipped and fell in the yard, it was as though all seven had taken a tumble. Their wails upset their plump mother, who would scurry from one daughter to the next, attempting not only to console them all but also to discover which had come to actual harm.

As they grew older, the seven Marías' problems multiplied seven-fold. In all, they suffered forty-nine cases of appendicitis, measles, and mumps, fourteen fractures, innumerable scrapes, sprains, head colds, and upset tummies, not to mention the terrible pandemic of toothaches brought on by the one who had a particular predilection for sweets. At school, each time a boy yanked on one María's braids, all the girls cringed in pain – and afterward they would seek their revenge by surrounding the culprit and spinning around him until he fainted from nausea.

As they entered their adolescence, their shared conflicts became more serious. Every time one María tried to remove a pimple, the other six felt the pinch and became annoyed. So it was that, in addition to shopping every week for food and supplies, Doña Toña had to acquire roses and peaches by the dozens to make ointments for the girls, hoping she'd be able to cut down the number of arguments that flared up with each blemish.

In truth, the whole village was amazed by the patience and constant good disposition that Doña Toña showed as she took her seven daughters, single file, to visit the doctor, or to hear Mass, or to attend school: they were always together. Mother had to cure their insomnia, alleviate their aches and discomforts, calm their angers, and satisfy each whim and curiosity: each month, the seven Marías suffered cramps through six menstrual cycles besides their own, an equal number of burns from pots and pans, and pricks from needles during evenings of sewing and knitting. Doña Toña was never too weary to attend to their needs. She seemed to possess the stamina and energy of seven women.

But the situation took a decided turn for the worse when one of the Marías fell in love with Juan. All seven lost their appetite, their heart rates soared, they found it impossible to concentrate when studying or sewing, and they ruined the dishes they cooked. Since only one had a genuine reason to suffer, the other six were beset by confusion. Doña Toña found herself trapped between deep sighs and fierce squabbling. Otherwise, her Marías spent their hours daydreaming, self-absorbed: they hummed tunes they'd made up as they sprawled out on the lawn or lounged in silk hammocks or drank lemonade in the old mosaic-tiled courtyard. Their mother devoutly prayed a rosary for each daughter every day.

After several weeks had passed, love-stricken María could stand it no longer. She went looking for Juan to confess her love, but she was so embarrassed when she came face-to-face with him that her six sisters could not summon the courage to get out of bed that morning. They were all flushed and tormented, so Doña Toña had to brew six pitchers of linden tea with chamomile blossoms before setting out to search for the missing María. Furious and desperate, their mother scoured the streets of the town in vain, because no one could tell her anything about her daughter's whereabouts.

When she returned home, she panicked: her six daughters were naked, smiling excitedly, and dancing around the house. They proclaimed they were feeling a strange tickling sensation all over the body, one that was especially pleasurable between their legs. Doña Toña lost her patience and her temper. She quickly ordered them all to take a cold bath and apply mint and eucalyptus leaf-compresses. María, in Juan's arms, reclining on the grass, shivered with cold, but that only caused her to embrace him with greater enthusiasm. Even under the effects of the cool water, the chorus of moans in Doña Toña's house made the walls quiver. The insults and blows that the mother rained down upon her daughters only seemed to make matters worse. The runaway María had resolved to resist with all her might the feelings and sensations that her sisters transmitted to her and, in spite of the pain all over her body, Juan's kisses and caresses relieved her discomfort.

Ultimately, however, the cumulative bruises of the sisters took their toll, and all seven Marías began to cry. Faced with María's unexpected tears, Juan was so terrified that he fled the village. His María was so hurt, yet simultaneously so rapturous, that she was incapable of running after him. The sight of him disappearing half-naked among the bushes brought on a profound depression. She shouted after him until her voice grew hoarse and her crying became uncontrollable.

Night had already fallen when Doña Toña found her. Her daughter's overwhelming sadness lessened her fury in the same way that the appetite of her young ones had diminished her own size, and so she merely tried to comfort the lovelorn María, helping her to walk home, offering neither reproach nor questions. Indeed, she profoundly regretted having struck her Marías for the first time, and swore to herself that it would be the last.

Once reunited with her seven Marías, Doña Toña didn't know which one to console first. María couldn't stop crying for her lost love, and the others suffered along with her. The tears were so copious Doña Toña gave up on the idea of absorbent towels and brought out her cups and jars, then a couple of rusty buckets to gather up the tears. The more María remembered Juan, the greater the distress she felt, and the more they all wept. Doña Toña finally emptied all her liquor, sauce, and vinegar bottles so she could fill them with tears. In a few days the whole town knew what was happening in the house and, motivated more by curiosity than by compassion, the village women showed up with more containers to contain the tears, which flowed without end.

It was by accident that Doña Toña decided to sell her daughters' tears. One of the neighbour women had carried away a jarful and, when she mistakenly drank out of it, she sank into disconsolate weeping all afternoon. After repeating the experiment, other women found it useful for when they had to attend a funeral or, as the shopkeeper's wife could attest, to blackmail her husband into giving her anything she wanted. Soon all the women in the village wanted to get their hands on a bottle or two of María Tears, to store away and have on hand for when the occasion warranted. Thus, they began to pay Doña Toña for her daughters' tears.

Not only did the tears of the Marías never cease, they became more and more abundant. María grieved perpetually for Juan, but she also bemoaned the sorry state in which her sisters found themselves. They, in turn, cried because of María's desolation and despondency, and also at their own plight. Their desperation mounted as they looked at each other and felt there was no escape from their misery. Doña Toña might have gone mad if not for the fact that such sobbing and screaming had driven her deaf a few days after the disaster began.

Gradually, news of Doña Toña's tear-store spread throughout the surrounding area. Men and women from everywhere started to arrive, hoping to obtain tears for occasional weeping. Lawyers came from as far away as the city, asking to purchase several bottles to help their clients perform heart-rending spectacles in front of a jury; adulterous women sought out the coveted fluid in order to convince their husbands of their undying love; men wishing to appear contrite in the eyes of offended lovers also yearned for a jar of their own... The processions leading to the tear-store were endless.

After so much crying, the Marías had begun to shrivel up. Doña Toña was frightened; she discovered that the more shrivelled her daughters became, the more fearful they felt, and the more they continued to cry. Numerous doctors were called upon to diagnose their condition. None of their elixirs helped. Doña Toña even hired the funniest circus clowns for miles around to make the Marías laugh, but when the clowns saw the unfortunate girls they too felt so sad that despair set in, and they could not muster a single amusing stunt. Neither the cleansing rituals of the most famous witch doctors nor the blessings of priests from neighbouring parishes could exert a calming effect. As a last resort, Doña Toña agreed to search for Juan, but she could not find him in any of the nearby towns. She offered all the money she had earned at her tear-store as a reward to anyone who could bring him to her house and reunite him with her daughter, but to no avail. Long lines of counterfeit Juans showed up, disheartening the unfortunate María, aggravating her propensity to cry.

Despite Doña Toña's efforts, the seven Marías grew more and more shriveled. Thus began the prayers of desperation, the impatience and anxiety, and, ultimately, the silent curses amid the fountain of tears. Doña Toña had them drink exotic fruit juices and rubbed sandalwood lotion on their bodies because she feared that her daughters had become bone-dry.

For ninety days and ninety nights she cared for her daughters, feeding them, anointing them, wrapping their bodies in sheets, towels, and bandages, but all was in vain. The incessant weeping suddenly caused the Marías, who were already shrivelled, to begin shrinking. Exasperated, Doña Toña shut down the tear-store and, ranting and screaming, drove away all the customers and curiosity seekers milling around her house.

No one heard any news of the family until, several days later, Doña Toña walked to the village for the sole purpose of asking the local craftsman to fashion seven small boxes made of mahogany. She ignored all comments and questions from the townsfolk, and she flatly refused to accept any company on her return trip home.

With her bare hands she dug a hole in the sunniest corner of her yard and in it, with the utmost care, she placed seven tiny containers, positioning them as close to each other as possible. Then she went to sit down in an old armchair on the terrace. She waited absently for time to erase her from the face of the earth and, along with her, any trace of what had happened in that place.

THE FIRST CUP
OF COFFEE

Nothing is more bitter than the first cup of coffee. I realized this just before dawn. It shouldn't seem strange to you; it's just the honest truth. I've never been good at lying. Today I drank coffee for the first time. Of course I'd seen and smelled it before. I liked the aroma a lot, but I had never imagined the taste would be so bitter.

Tobías wouldn't let me have any because he'd promised my dad. He always said it stains your teeth. Give me a break. As if at this point that could matter. Dad thought ladies shouldn't drink anything except "tea, Greta, and milk." Can you imagine? With this flat, dark, round face of mine and he still named me Greta. It seems like a joke. He was a stubborn old bastard, and strict, too. I never dared disobey him. Then, to top it off, he made me marry Tobías, which was all I needed to make my life even more miserable. I don't know how I could stand it all, but it was my fault anyway for letting him push me around. And for being so dumb. Could you pour me a little more, please?

Excuse me for talking so much to you, but since there's nobody else around … I'm tired. The bus ride here took eight hours, and ever since this afternoon I've been looking high and low for my childhood friend, Claudia, but I can't find her anywhere. There's a park now where her house used to be. I could see it if she'd just left and somebody else moved in, or if they'd turned it into a little corner store, maybe even an office or something. What I don't understand is why they tore the house down. Why it's a park now. We've got more open spaces and air here than we need. Dry, dusty air that smells like goat and cow shit. It's always been like that. That's the problem: "people live in this air and get their fill of this air and then they don't think like people any more but like animals," as Claudia used to say. And she said smelling shit was bad for your brain and I should leave before what happened to everybody else happened to me, and I would end up stuck here until the day I died. But the way I see it, leaving was worse than staying. I know that now.

I was sure I would find her in her house today. I could see the surprised look on her face when she saw me show up after all these years, so overweight. You know, I wasn't like this at all when I went off with Tobías, no way. But what can I do about it now? When you've got money and you're unhappy you get fat, and unfortunately Tobías had lots of dough. He was always flaunting it. That's exactly why I brought Claudia the presents he gave me, because I don't want anything of his. I have to hand them over to her, but nobody knows where she is. They say the park's been there quite a while now. The people I knew have all left or passed away. I know because I went to the cemetery to see if I could find a tombstone with Claudia's name on it, just to make sure, so I could quit worrying about it, but instead of hers I discovered plenty of others I wasn't expecting. It's like death has not left my side for the past several hours.

I hate cops. That's why I didn't want to stay there. They ask you a lot of questions and they accuse you of anything they can think of for no good reason. What happened to Tobías was not my fault. I took away with me only what was mine so they couldn't pin anything else on me. Sooner or later things were going to go against him, and I told him they would. That game of his was really dangerous. The only thing I regret now is all the time it took me to think of a way to help fate along. Both of us would have suffered less.

I tried the coffee but couldn't bring myself to finish it before I left. I just set the cup down on the table, half full. That was the first time since I married Tobías that I was able to leave a dish dirty. I even felt like taking out all the plates and smearing them with hot sauce and oil and butter and jam and whatnot, just for the pleasure of not hearing him scream at me about it, so I could feel like the house was all mine. But I had no time for that. All I did was gather up some of my stuff and toss it into a suitcase along with the things I had saved up for Claudia, and then I headed for the station. The sun was about to rise and I was sleepy when I arrived to take the first bus here. I thought I would rest during the trip but I didn't even close my eyes thinking about what had happened and the way things would be from now on.

Sure, go ahead, have a tequila with me. What's the harm?

"Greta, get my bath running; Greta, get dinner ready; Greta, rub my back, tie me a knot in this tie, sew on this button." Tobías never gave me a moment's peace. He wouldn't let me leave the house by myself, as though they would kidnap me or something. But look at me. Nobody would even give me a second glance. Just the day before yesterday he went with me to the market, only to make sure nothing improper would happen. As if I would even be in the mood for anything like that. And every day, before he left for work, he locked up the coffee pot, of course. That was his obsession: another way to control me and assert his *power*. What power? The guy was useless for everything. That's why he'd shut himself up in his room at night to play with his gun.

The first time I saw him do it was on our wedding night. I was pretty scared, naturally. I didn't love him to begin with. Even his money didn't interest me. He got undressed, helped me get undressed as well, and there I was, feeling nervous and a bit disgusted, and then we climbed into bed. He put his hand on my tummy and began to run it down toward my legs so he could open them up. He lay down on top of me and I could feel his breath in my ear and on my neck, I could feel him fumbling clumsily, if you know what I mean, but as soon as I closed my eyes and took a deep breath, hoping the pain and discomfort Claudia had warned me about wouldn't be so bad, he hopped up and went over to the dresser. I was going to ask him what was wrong but before I could say anything he took out the gun and put it in his mouth. He was about to pull the trigger when I covered my face with my hands, expecting the worst. After an agonizing moment of silence I heard a single *click*. And then, nothing. Once again, nothing happened.

The rest of the night he didn't even come near me. He put the gun back in the drawer and went to sleep on a sofa. At first he was tossing and turning. He couldn't sleep, and neither could I. I wasn't going to close my eyes, are you kidding me? All I did was pray for somebody to come get me out of there and take me back to my house. I'd rather have been with my dad and put up with him. At least I was used to his ways. But it didn't take me long to realize I wouldn't be able to escape.

The next day he took me to town and bought me some really nice dresses and some jewelry. He even looked proud to be walking beside me. But he didn't take his eyes off me for a second, heaven forbid, and even when I had to go to the restroom he stood waiting for me right outside the door. Back then, around these parts everybody figured he was the finest catch, as they say, so my dad was sure he was doing the right thing for me. "Tobías is a fancy man, Greta," my dad told me the day we said goodbye. "At least you won't be lacking for anything, and you'll look like a queen at his side." And Dad was right on that score: he did have good taste in clothes, and he liked to walk down the street holding my arm and introducing me to his friends saying, "This is my woman. Eat your heart out." And he loved to shout and yell, he sure did, only I found that out much later. I figured some day he'd bust a gut screaming his drunken head off.

The worst thing of all was that he'd never let me go out alone. For the first few days that was understandable. All I wanted to do was get out of there, go find Claudia and ask her if we could leave together or if she'd let me stay at her house, or whatever. Then time went by and I got used to staying home and finding little chores to keep myself busy. Little by little I felt less like running away.

Whenever Tobías came home drunk he cried and begged me not to abandon him. He said he wanted to make me happy but just didn't know how. He begged me to believe that he was really trying. That was touching at the beginning. He'd curl up in my arms like a little baby. I started to become fond of him in spite of his refusing to let me go out alone and locking the door whenever he left the house. To prove that he wanted to make me happy, he bought me a TV so I didn't get bored while I was waiting for him. That was nice, you know? And yet I felt lonely. I yearned for more. See, at night... How can I even say this? Oh, well, who cares? All he did was lie next to me, just sleep and that was it, you understand? He never touched me.

"Don't you want to have kids?" I asked him one day. Man, did I regret that. He said if I thought he wasn't man enough to make me a bunch of kids, he'd show me how wrong I was, and he hit me. He pulled down his pants and...nothing. He couldn't do it, just like on our wedding night. He hit me so hard he had to take me to the hospital because my head split open. Look, I've got the scar right here. And no hair grows around it.

The doctor wanted to know what happened to me and asked me if I wanted to press charges against my husband, but I didn't dare. Tobías had such an expression on his face, he looked so desperately sorry, and I really didn't want to get mixed up with the cops. I already told you I hate cops. So I swore to the doctor that I'd fallen down the stairs. He didn't believe me, but what did it matter? After that Tobías gave me a gold bracelet with my name on one side and his on the other and a little doggie so I wouldn't feel so lonely at home. I didn't want to embarrass him, so I didn't bring up the idea of kids again. I named the puppy Nicolás, and for a while things were okay.

Since I would spend all day at home knitting doilies, embroidering our pillows, doing housework – he always wanted everything to be spotless – and watching TV, well, little by little I lost my figure. I feared Tobías would force me to go on a diet. He had been so proud of my looks when we first got married, after all. But to my surprise, he let me be. Besides, by that time I was not exactly a young lady any more. Tobías would go with me to buy new clothes and take me to the market, and he kept giving me little pieces of silver jewelry, sometimes gold, but he wouldn't let me go with him anywhere else. He was probably embarrassed to be seen with me. He didn't invite his buddies home anymore – which actually was just fine because he had been impossible when they were around, grabbing my ass with his grubby hands right in front of everybody, watching all the gestures, the looks, so that none of them would dare even speak to me – and sometimes he wouldn't even come home to sleep. Nicolás would sit next to me, and I'd stroke his little head, and we'd just stay there like that until the sun came up.

It was around that time that Tobías stopped playing Russian roulette with that damned gun of his. I didn't say a thing, because he looked happy, peaceful. Perhaps he was having an affair? Knowing what I knew about him, it was unlikely. But just in case, I never asked. "You are my saint," he'd say when he got home. I wouldn't even look at him. All I began to live for was to dream about returning here. The only thing that broke the monotony was being with my dog. I fed him the same food I gave Tobías, when he wasn't looking, of course, and I played with him for hours on end. I kept him shampooed and perfectly groomed. I knitted him a sweater for cold weather. I wish my dad could have known him. My dad was ill-tempered and stubborn, but he was very fond of animals, he sure was. And I know Claudia would have liked Nicolás, too. But the dog died of old age, and I never had a chance to come here. Tobías wouldn't let me.

I got so used to going out with my husband that early this morning in the bus station I felt lost and I almost started to cry. Walking among strange people without anybody to guide me, I felt very insecure. I was dying to get here. I thought that as soon as I found Claudia everything would be all right, but as you can see I haven't located her yet, and this place has changed so much I feel more lost than ever.

My dad? My dad died a long time ago. He was my only family, but even knowing that, Tobías would not let me go to his burial. He made up all kinds of excuses not to come. He even said he "couldn't miss work." Damn it, you mean my dad had to wait for Tobías's "vacation" to come along before he could die? It's not as if we ever went on any trips. I've got to be honest with you: it was very hard for me to forgive him. But in spite of it all, in the end I did. I also ended up forgiving him for beating me, you know, and for not letting me drink coffee or go out alone. But what he did to Nicolás the Second – *that* was unforgivable.

When Nicolás died I was terribly sad. All I did was cry, I even stopped eating for a week or so. None of Tobías's presents could console me, until one day in the market Tobías bought me a rabbit in a cage. He was white with red eyes and a pink nose, pretty run-of-the-mill, I guess, but I thought he was awful cute. When I was a little girl, at home we had a bunch of rabbits and I loved to feed them and take care of them. So I felt really happy.

In the morning, while I did the cleaning or cooking, Nicolás the Second stayed in his cage, but in the afternoon I always took him out and put him on my lap to watch television. During these past few months I wouldn't even wait up for Tobías, because I got used to him arriving in the wee hours of the morning. I stopped worrying about him and asking him to install a phone in the house or buy me a cell phone so he could let me know where he was. As if the master of the house was going to listen! Not a chance. Not even when I told him that, if there was ever an emergency, I would have no way of getting hold of him. "Emergency? Here? Don't be ridiculous, what could happen?" he replied, and simply kept on doing whatever he pleased. After a while it didn't matter to me whether he came or went, as long as the pantry was full and the TV was on. While I watched my soap operas or did my embroidery I chatted with Nicolás the Second, who was really a fantastic listener and looked at me as though he understood everything I told him. I'd often speak to him about my dad and about Claudia, too. About how things used to be when I was young. About everything I missed.

But as it happened, three days ago, that son-of-a-bitch Tobías – excuse me, but I guess this tequila is going to my head, because I'm not used to drinking – came home really late, drunk as a skunk and hungry as a wolf, and instead of waking me up to cook something for him, like he usually did, he got it into his head to... Just remembering it makes me want to cry. That bastard threw Nicolás the Second into a stew pot. He broke his neck and tossed him into the pot to have him for breakfast, he said. Does that make any sense to you? No, right? It doesn't make any sense at all! But that's what he did, and that's what he said, and he made a big racket walking out of the kitchen because he was so drunk he was stumbling, and that's how I could tell something bad was going on in the first place.

That was the first time I ever held him responsible for anything. "Why'd you have to kill my little bunny? He was already old! Did you think that if you ate him you could get it up? Not even a miracle would get it up, *cabrón*!" Whew, forgive me, I never use that sort of language. But I was so angry that I can't even remember what else I screamed at him or why I didn't bust a gut yelling at the top of my lungs. All I knew was that I was not about to put up with that damned Tobías for another instant. Nicolás the Second was my friend, he was my only company. Of course Tobías hit me, but I didn't cry. Look, I've still got the bruises on my arms, and my lip is a bit swollen, see? But I swear I didn't shed a single tear. I kept repeating what I thought of him until I suppose he finally got tired of listening to me and he gave up. So guess what he did. Well, he went straight to his room to play Russian roulette again. The gun only had one bullet in it, and unfortunately it wasn't his turn to die. He was spared again. I don't think I'd ever been so furious in all my life.

After he left I felt relieved but then the wait turned out to be terrible because this time it took him a day and a half to come back home. And all of a sudden I started wondering. What if he didn't come back at all? What would I do then? I had to come up with a plan.

I buried Nicolás the Second in a large flowerpot, where else? The backyard was all cement, with not so much as a square foot of lawn. What was the use of having a big house if there was no yard? I kept telling Tobías that, but he refused to give in. He said there'd be a lot of dirt and dust getting into the rooms and it would attract bugs. Bugs? Are you kidding me? As if here, in this very town where we met, there hadn't been any.

To make a long story short, when Tobías returned he brought me a pearl necklace as a gift. He must have forgotten that I already had three of them. And what good were they anyway, if I couldn't put them on to go anywhere? I told him, "I don't care about your presents, you're not a man." I screamed and threw the necklace out of the bathroom window. Of course I took care to stand close to the door so I could slam it shut before he could get in to hit me. He stayed there for quite a while, waiting for me to come out, but I sat down on the floor and thought that, as far as I was concerned, we could just stay there for hours. Finally he got tired and went out again when night began to fall. I wasn't scared then. I knew he would return.

Okay, let's have one more tequila, but this will be my last one for tonight.

I pretended to be asleep when I heard him open up the front door, but I was certain he was drunk because he stumbled again. He came into the bedroom and just stood there next to me. I wasn't stupid enough to open my eyes. I thought that if I did, he would hit me for sure, because he'd been wanting to. I heard him take off his pants and felt him sit down on his side of the bed. Then he opened his dresser drawer. For a second I felt like warning him about the gun, but it was too late to change my mind. You won't tell anybody, will you? While he had been out I decided to search everywhere for the rest of those blessed bullets so I could help him out with that game he liked so much. I put in four more: that way there was still one empty space. If fate really and truly wanted him to survive, he would.

On second thought, do give me a little more. Just half, though. This really is my last one.

I pulled the blanket up over me and started to say the Lord's Prayer. I wasn't halfway through it when I heard the shot. I heard him fall to the floor and tried to get up to see exactly what had happened, but I was too afraid. Then I remembered I'd left everything in God's hands, and therefore whatever took place had only been His will, and that was a big relief. I went over to get a look at him and take his house keys so I could let myself out. And guess what? This time he did have it up. Can you believe that? I could hardly believe it myself when I saw it.

I took his key ring and on it I found the key to the drawer where he kept the coffee pot, so I went and made myself a cup. I had lost interest in the taste of coffee a long time earlier – I just settled for the aroma – but at that precise moment I felt an overwhelming urge to taste it. Anyway, I gathered up the presents for Claudia and a few of my clothes, opened the door, and headed for the station as fast as I could to catch the first bus that would bring me here. I didn't even look back at Tobías.

That's why I'm here. I don't imagine anybody will think of looking for me. He died by his own hand, after all. What will I do if I don't find Claudia? I looked for her all afternoon and into the evening. My feet still ache from all that walking. It's ridiculous that there's a park now on the spot where her house used to be. Tomorrow, when I'm feeling better, I'm gonna go ask around and find out what happened. Right now my head is spinning. What? No, thanks, no coffee. I told you, there's nothing more bitter.

STILL WATCHING;
WATCHING, STILL

I shouldn't have bought the newspaper, but I couldn't help myself. I folded it to place it under my arm and still be able to hold Rodrigo, who had fallen asleep. I walked back home and closed the door, but didn't feel safe until I was in my bedroom and put my son down to continue his nap. I closed the curtains after carefully checking no one was spying on us – that no one was outside looking at me, or for me, even though no one has for years – and sat down at the end of the bed, my foot tapping on the floor without me wanting it to. This constant restlessness, this impossibility to be at peace – I inherited from Father.

I opened the newspaper and read the article swiftly, as if I was being timed on it, not really knowing why I was in such rush. I was about to read it once more when Rodrigo woke up. Time flew by, and I didn't think about it again until now. It's dark; Rodrigo shouldn't wake up until the morning. Such an easy child! Sleeps like I haven't done in years. And as I watch his chest going up and down and enjoy his skin's smell of chamomile and lavender – the warmth of his body curled up against mine – I try to remember *him*. Father.

My memories of us together are scarce. I have a much better recollection of the things that he didn't do. He never took me to school. He was never there for my birthday. At the beginning I thought it was because he didn't love me. I believed the girls at my school who teased me saying that he had abandoned me and Mother. That perhaps he had another family. Mother's silence about his absences was sharp as a knife; from early on I learned to not ask questions.

Mother used to cry at night, and also in the shower, hoping the water would wash off her anguish. But her skin was a familiar territory, and I could read her body – her slightly curved back, her silent steps – the way people read a map. She didn't tell me what was going on, but she couldn't fool me. Thinking of Rodrigo and the questions he might ask when he grows up, I revisit my endlessly hushed childhood and rehearse possible answers. Answers that my dear old Nacha would like, such as "But we must feel very proud." Bullshit.

I have no energy to read the article again. Instead, I curl up beside Rodrigo. I *do* remember Father lying down just like this, right beside me, when he paid us a surprise visit. I remember his wet, long hair, his breathing – tired, devoid of peace. There was always dirt under his nails, no matter how hard he scrubbed his hands. They smelled of the soap Mother used to buy, and I knew he had scrubbed them because the points of his fingers were reddish, irritated. I used to open my eyes and explore his hands, comparing them to mine. Their size and shape. Our identical thumbs. Father's hands holding me turned my world into an upside-down desert landscape where I was kept warm at night and then froze up with his absence as soon as the sun came out.

I close my eyes and listen. Thousands of insects sing their night song. *In this country not even the bugs let you be at peace*, he complained. But I've always liked their humming. Our house was so quiet that the bugs reminded me we were alive.

Rodrigo stretches his body and puts his little leg on top of mine. I caress it and realize how long it has become. His foot is almost as big as my hand. The desire to keep him small like this, cuddling beside me, breaks like a wave against my chest and threatens to drown me. I hold back the urge to cry. Father liked to measure his feet with mine. He said that's how he knew I was his daughter: that I would always take firm steps forward. He was wrong.

I was less than ten years old when he died. Mom and I had moved to the countryside, and he had not visited us even once. Other people came, people I didn't know, who didn't stay long and also spoke in hushed voices. We were surrounded by mountains, and I don't know if it was because of how cold it was at night, but no insect could ever be heard. Just the wind pounding against the windows. Drafts so violent they seemed to want to evict us. An omen, perhaps? A warning we were incapable of deciphering.

During that period, Mother used to travel back to the city quite often. She left early in the morning and returned late at night, and I was under the care of Nacha, our neighbour, who had no family and came to stay with me. Or took me to her house, which was an enormous hacienda with endless hallways, spacious rooms with thick walls, and storage areas that we explored together and played hide-and-seek in. I didn't attend school anymore. Mother said what I needed to learn was not being taught there anyway, so Nacha became my teacher. She taught me all about growing food, taking care of animals, which herbs were good to cure an ailment.

Mother slept very little. The dark circles around her eyes told the story of nights spent pacing ceaselessly around the house. Praying. Not a good sign – she'd never prayed before.

The news that changed it all forever arrived by surprise on the first page of the same newspaper I bought today. Father had fatally wounded the General. In exchange, he received all the bullets his body could take. Seventy-two. I remember the number not only because it was published, but because it's also the year I was born in. There was a picture of his swollen black-and-white face covered in dark stains; his eyes half-open. On bad days this is the image of his I remember with most sharpness. I have tried to recover the sound of his voice – of his whispers, rather – but it's been futile. All I can evoke is the warmth of his breath; the insects humming softly in the background. And ever since Nacha died, all I have left is Rodrigo. I sink my nose in the back of his neck to stop myself from crying, but I can't.

There were many more casualties that September. Father was not the only dissident participating in the assassination, but he was considered the leader. In a place without rules or rights, a tyrant's followers, even after his death, are ruthless. Mother knew it and, in spite of that – or, who knows, maybe *because* of that – left shortly after Father died. For our own safety, she didn't say where she was going, or when she'd be back. She asked Nacha to take care of me. I wanted to go with her, begged and pleaded to no avail. It was a cool October morning when she left. The sun was shining and no clouds were to be seen. Nature has its own way to mock despair. I needed a storm to erupt right there and then. A sign that, somehow, I was not utterly alone. But I wasn't granted such mercy.

I've always wondered whether I'm fortunate or cursed because the soldiers who were looking for Mother "and her accomplices" didn't find me. I may very well be the only survivor of that group of people the regime called "rebels" and "enemies of the nation." Little did it matter that I was a child. Only later did I understand that Nacha's hide-and-seek games had not not really been games.

My memories of the day they came looking for us are blurry. Nacha gave me a couple of pills – she, who was so against pills – and asked me to hide in one of our favourite spots in the barn. I fell asleep. I woke up when everything was over and the only evidence of the unwelcome visit was the hacienda in disarray. The house where Mother and I had lived was burning. Nacha's face, swollen. She had several bruises and difficulty walking; they hit her to force her to talk. I have no clue how she knew they were coming. How she found out just in time. After that day, the wind stopped feeling like a threat and became my voice. It screamed for me. It banged with fury while I sunk deeper and deeper into an even more painful silence.

Mother's name is still on the list of the disappeared.

I kiss Rodrigo's forehead and think of Nacha. She brought me back to the city, enrolled me in school. Never ceased repeating that my parents had fought so I could live in a better country. Bullshit. *No country's good for a girl who's left totally alone, Nacha.* I never said it aloud; I didn't want to hurt her. But the truth is that this place isn't better than before. And the freedom I inherited is dark and clammy, like blood. It hasn't even helped me learn how to speak loudly inside my own house.

Today's newspaper featured an article on the upcoming unveiling of a statue of Father. The President himself will lead the ceremony. I smile bitterly and examine my feet. They'll never reach Father's shadow.

Which photo did they use as a model to sculpt his face for the statue? I wonder if it's the one they've published ad nauseam since our so-called return to democracy – the one Mother took shortly after they met, where his locks looked as if they had a life of their own. She had it with her when she left.

What would Father say now, seeing himself in bronze, his name on a plaque, flowers adorning our flag placed at his feet? Did he like birds? I don't know. But he'll be surrounded by them in the park. They'll defecate all over his statue. In this country, even the most sacred things become shitty.

I imagine what would happen if I were to show up at the ceremony to tell everyone who I am. His story, my story – my side of history. Or perhaps it'd be easier to take Rodrigo and leave. Start a new life somewhere.

Two things I'm thankful for. One: Rodrigo's father chose not to be a part of our lives. Two: I know where Nacha's buried. I'll always have something dear in this land, yet nothing holds me here.

The insects bring me back to reality. *Forgive me, Nacha. Even though I promised you I would, I cannot lift my voice.*

Now that Father has become a statue he might understand me. He, too, will be standing still, watching life go by. But we'll forever remain different because, as I watch Rodrigo sleep (he has Father's curls!), I realize my son's little hands are an extension of the ocean: my entire world fits into them. And I need nothing more.

POLAR BEARS
ARE BULLSHIT

"The pancakes didn't come out round, but they taste good," Henry whined.

The dirty utensils and some flour and milk on the floor nettled her. This *had* to happen on top of another sleepless night, when she was already going to be late for work. That morning her boss had an important meeting, and he needed her at the office earlier than usual.

She had warned Henry the night before: "Dad, tomorrow's an important day at the agency. I'll have to leave early." Now she had to mop the kitchen floor before leaving. "I don't appreciate this," she said. "Just so you know."

Henry kept silent and tried to caress her head, but she moved away.

"And don't feel sorry for me either," she said softly, as she bent down to pick up a bucket to fill it with water.

"You obviously didn't get any sleep. You look terrible."

"Thanks," she answered, focusing on the mop and the new anti-bacterial multi-surface cleaning liquid she had bought a couple of days before.

"Why don't you put on a different skirt?"

No answer.

"You can't go out like that. You look like crap," he said as he poured maple syrup onto his pancakes and took a bite. For a second, the lavender smell of the floor cleaner made her feel better – helped her not to think about food.

"They're getting cold, Maggie."

She looked at her watch and shrugged. There was no time to sit down and have breakfast with him anyway.

"Invite Mr. Lee to eat with you," she said, while rinsing the mop and putting it away.

Henry looked down, purse-mouthed, staring at his pancakes. "You're the one who says I shouldn't eat those things because they're fattening. I don't get you."

She walked out of the kitchen to her bedroom. Henry followed, holding his plate in one hand and a fork in the other. He stopped at the door.

"Don't you ever get tired, Maggie?"

"Tired of what?"

"Of waiting."

Maggie slammed her bedroom door shut, but her father didn't give up.

"I'd be ashamed if I were still a virgin at your age," he said, raising his voice to make sure she heard him. "You're going to dry up."

She kept still until she heard his receding footsteps. He'd never been that brazen, that brutal. Why did he have to say things that way? She looked at herself in the mirror and fixed her hair. It was true: the grey skirt and the blouse with the ruffles did make her look heavy, but she was in too much of a rush to stop and look for something else in the closet. Besides, if she did it would mean acknowledging that he was right.

Her stomach churned. She hadn't eaten. The smell of pancakes and maple syrup teased her appetite. She blotted her eyes with a tissue and applied more makeup to her face. She half opened the door to her room and stuck out her head:

"I'm happy just the way I am!" she stated, then slammed the door.

She splashed perfume on her neck and arms, put the pink bottle in her purse, checked her cell phone before turning it off – five text messages waiting already. "Better hurry than waste time reading them," she whispered to herself – and, after taking a deep breath, finally gathered strength to walk into the hall.

Henry was standing by the front door, holding his plate of pancakes. As he chewed, he said:

"If you were happy, you'd at least have changed your perfume."

Maggie felt like crying, but stifled the urge.

"Why do you treat me like this? Why?"

"You disgust me."

"Nobody's forcing you to stay in this house, Dad."

Henry walked back into the kitchen, and Maggie moved quickly toward the door, not looking back.

From the table Henry heard the sound of the apartment door opening. He was startled to hear Maggie shout, "Mr. Lee! You scared me!"

Maggie walked as fast as she could down the hall to the stairs, without saying goodbye. Mr. Lee always showed up without warning, at the most inconvenient of times. Maybe he was spying on them, she thought. He and Henry were probably having a good laugh about the whole incident – laughing at her – and more than ever Maggie detested Mr. Lee. Having him so close by with that permanent little smile on his lips, quiet and discreet, but always scrutinizing the slightest gesture, dissecting every word she and her father said, lighting up one cigarette after another. Always smiling. Her living room smelled of tobacco every day. Every evening she opened the windows. So many times she had lost track.

She walked into the street, certain that when she returned, not only would she find a mess in the kitchen, but she could see butts filling the ashtray, syrup stuck to the dishes in the sink, ants gathering in the grease, and empty beer cans on the table by the TV. She thought again about Raymond: he didn't smoke or drink, and soon he would come for her. Maggie looked at her ringless fingers, trying to imagine the ring Ray was going to give her.

She was about to turn the corner when she realized she'd forgotten to check the mail. She checked it every morning before going to work. She turned back, and crossed the fingers of her left hand before opening the mailbox. Maybe this time the letter would be there. That would be the finest excuse ever for arriving late to an important meeting.

She stuck her right hand into the mailbox, feeling the cold metal and, at the back, an envelope. She touched it gingerly. It didn't have a stamp. She quickly withdrew her hand with a quick motion and examined the envelope. It was addressed to her; her typed name was on the front. The type looked familiar. She read the message:

See how it's no use to keep on waiting?

Maggie knew her father could be cruel, but this note was too much. She ripped it up, letting little pieces scatter to the floor. She walked back to the street, determined to tell her father to move out of the apartment. She'd tell him after work. No wonder he'd taken the trouble to fix her favourite breakfast. Maybe Mr. Lee was in on the whole thing. How could Mr. Lee, his yellowed teeth and his stained pajamas, be mean to her? When she worked every day so that he could drink half the beer she bought for her father! She was going to get rid of the two of them.

The pavement was wet from the rain. To protect her best pair of shoes, the ones with cute heels that she wore only to special meetings, she took care not to step in any puddles, and when she arrived at the bus stop it was a relief to see that no one was waiting there. She had never liked anyone seeing her cry.

She was forty-five minutes late and that was too late. The streets were so congested. Unable to bear the thought of a reprimand, incapable of lying to her boss, she got off the bus several blocks before her stop, not knowing where to go. A sudden sensation of freedom seemed strange, uncomfortable. When her stomach started to churn again once more she got up the nerve to go into a café. She chose a small table in the rear, and sat down with her back to the window. She asked for an order of pancakes "with lots of syrup" and a glass of cold milk. And after that, a slice of apple pie. She touched her belly – four folds of skin formed when she was sitting. Maybe she shouldn't eat so much, after all. But Henry had no right to criticize her. Certainly not her loyalty. What did he know about promises? He had never kept one. Not even the one he made about keeping the house clean.

She paid the check and decided to go to the zoo.

She walked without stopping at any particular cage, making a special effort to avoid the polar bears' pond. She'd seen them too many times. They were Raymond's favourites. The evening before he left "in search of better opportunities for both of us," he'd promised to come back with an engagement ring and a big white teddy bear. And with enough money to go far away. Just the two of them. That day, he had unbuttoned her blouse for the first time. She liked the feel of his large hands cupping her breasts, the warmth of his tongue on her nipples. She remembered him every night before going to sleep. Looking at the white, majestic bears without him by her side would be too much. They would make her remember the rest: that she had stopped him from undressing her; that when his fingers slid under her white panties her heart beat faster, which she had never been able to get to happen by herself; that she had let his fingers continue, and when she felt them inside her, instead of letting out a moan she had screamed, closed her legs, and moved away. That's when he had promised the ring, the teddy bear, the big house, the kids. And she had said yes. She'd be his wife when he returned. She'd made him swear that he'd return. When he'd left he was solemn, sad perhaps? Yes, maybe his goodbye had been curt, but, "That way, goodbyes hurt less."

"You've still got time," Henry had told her just the day before. "Why don't you look for someone before your hair turns grey?" She regretted having made her father her only confidant. What did he know about true love? Letting him move in with her after he had retired was a big mistake. How comfortable, how marvellous it would be to return home and not find him there. It would be better if he'd just disappear, she thought, as she took a seat on a bench beside the duck pond. The quacks blended with the laughter of children who were throwing breadcrumbs into the water. Orange beaks plunged beneath the surface.

"I wish I were a duck so I wouldn't have to wear high heels," she thought as she removed her shoes, which had already left red marks around her instep. Her feet ached too much. "Those shoes are not good for walking," Henry had said when she'd shown them to him. Now she didn't know what bothered her the most: the fact that he had crushed her enthusiasm over her new shoes, or that he had been right. Perhaps it was she, Maggie, who was not good for walking. Or, for anything other than being alone. She gazed at her feet, swollen, ungainly, where her body began, and realized that it was through her feet that loneliness invaded her. No one could ever get rid of the feeling of being abandoned, because loneliness lived in the feet, the last things to separate from a mother at birth and the only body part that cannot be united, melded with another human being. Eyes closed, she imagined loneliness as a liquid rising up from the ankles, paralyzing her knees, numbing her groin and, reaching her chest, smothering her will to live.

A shudder of cold startled her. She stood up and forced herself to walk over to the polar bear pond. She didn't want to, but she had to see them. Taking short steps, her knees were weak, her forehead damp. She would treat herself to something tasty to eat as a reward for her forbearance. She caught a glimpse of them through a small crowd. In front of them, she realized she couldn't remember Raymond's voice. She closed her eyes and tried. The promise, the goodbye. Nothing. If she thought of his hands it was because she had replaced them with her own every night. Because she needed to, or from force of habit. It didn't matter. She felt ashamed. She made herself sick. But she took in a deep breath, holding to her spot for what seemed like a long while.

By mid-afternoon, with her shoes in one hand and a sandwich in the other, she left the zoo. She didn't want to return home so early and walked several blocks without deciding where to go. Clouds, clustered over the buildings, threatened to open up and dump a drenching rain, but that did not worry her. People were walking at a brisk pace beside her, staring at her bare feet. Maggie did not care.

She plodded along, feeling her thighs chafe at every step. Only when heavy drops of rain struck her head did she put on her shoes and seek shelter under a canvas awning in front of a small convenience store, and then in a bar.

The place being almost empty, she felt safe. She downed a shot of rum to warm up, but the rain wasn't slacking off, so she ordered another to kill time. After that, another. She lost track of the drinks. She looked at the empty tables around her and began to cry.

"Can I help you?" the waiter inquired, offering her another rum.

Maggie gulped down the rum in one swallow, paid the bill, got to her feet and said to the waiter:

"Polar bears are bullshit, don't you think?"

Maggie tilted her head back as she walked out into the dark street, heading for home. Taking the bus never occurred to her. The water trickled from her hair down her neck and her back, down her shoulders to her chest, until her wet blouse stuck to her body and her shoes made a squishy sound against the pavement. She stopped to search inside her purse. She felt her phone and was tempted by habit to turn it on, to check her messages, but she didn't. Her pink perfume was at the bottom of her purse. She took it out and threw it into a sidewalk trash can.

The rain had stopped when she got to the front door and she saw that Henry was still awake. His window was the only one with a light on. She opened the glass door to the lobby. The letter was no longer scattered on the floor. She paused before the door to her own place but suddenly went to her neighbour's. She pressed the door-bell and held it until Mr. Lee appeared.

"I just wanted to tell you to go fuck yourself."

Mr. Lee, not knowing what to say, stood in a daze, watching her, barefoot and soaking wet, go down the hall to her apartment.

Henry was ready for her. "Where were you?"

"Better yet, where are you going to be starting tomorrow, because I don't want you here," she said sternly.

The smell, the stench of cigarette smoke and stale beer took her by surprise but she said nothing about it, nor about the beer cans on the table by the TV. She saved herself the trouble of going into the kitchen. She assumed that the leftovers from breakfast, lunch and dinner were waiting for her in the sink. She was in no mood to wash even a single dish. Never again.

Her temples were about to explode.

She shut herself in her bedroom and undressed in front of the mirror. Her makeup had become two dark circles around her eyes. With her hair drenched, her head seemed too small for her body. The flabby, white skin bunched up below her breasts and her wide thighs disgusted her. She heard water running in the bathroom. Her father was drawing her a bath. She slipped on a robe and stepped into the hall. She didn't look up to see Henry, who was watching her from the kitchen door.

She felt an almost unbearable burning as she put her feet into the hot water, but she forced herself to climb in anyway. The clear water became clouded with dirt. Maggie scrubbed her body with soap until the heat became so concentrated in her head that she couldn't go on. She dunked her face in the grey, scummy water and remembered the ducks. She held her breath until anguish made her straighten up. She was ashamed of her cowardice and began hitting the tile wall with her fists. She could hear her father's footsteps up and down the hall. She bit her lip so she wouldn't say anything and waited until the water, too, was completely still.

Finally, after staring at Henry's old-fashioned razor blade, she picked it up and held it in her hands, wondering, and then suddenly certain that she would not show up for work the next morning.

Henry was waiting for her by the door when Maggie finally came out. She saw relief in his face.

"I left a cup of tea on your dresser. We can talk tomorrow," he said. His voice caressing, the way it had been when she was a little girl needing to calm down after a nightmare.

Maggie nodded, still drying her hair with a damp towel.

"By the way," she said, averting her eyes, "just for laughs, I hid your razor, I maybe even threw it out."

AZTEC WOMAN

They came and took everything. What was ours, our children's – what the wise men had given us. They ran off with all that was beautiful, and destroyed the rest. They taught us how to speak in this language that tastes of foreign skin. They turned our waters into rivers of blood: *our own blood* spilled without reason, without anyone to be nourished from its strength. They thought death would make us docile. No. We tamed death long ago.

I am not Maria, nor Guadalupe, nor Marina, and even if they call me by any of those names, I know none of them is mine. They stole my name when they silenced my gods, when they killed my parents, and I've been looking for it ever since. That's why I came here. To claim it. I don't care what they do to me. Nothing can be worse. My world is no more.

He was already old; he couldn't defend himself. My trained hand and sharp obsidian knife were quicker than his voice yapping for help. Help is what we deserved, what we were desperate to receive. They took it all away, even the hope of having someone hear our screams and come to our aid. He deserved to be, like us, alone in his fear. The knife entered his stomach, and when he tried to cover the wound with his hands I opened his neck like those of the gobblers that hang upside down in the market square. He fell to the floor and, before he finished drowning, I said to him, loud and clear so that he would hear me: "Father, I accuse myself of not loving your God like the ones you robbed from me, and of not being able to continue living with a name that has erased my voice. Amen."

I opened his chest and my hand dived into his body. The sound of my fingers searching that warm territory reminded me of the rivers flowing in the spring, of the water that sprouts from the earth's guts when the sun is shining. I finally took it out: his heart, a new-born animal unable to breathe. The palm of my hand became its nest. A shiny heart, shiny like the gold they came looking for, which cost us so many dear lives. I didn't turn around to see the Father's face: he was not my father... I don't know why he forced me to call him that. I watched his heart slow down between my fingers and, crying for all that I had lost, I told him: "I don't care what they do to me. This is who I am."

PAGANINI FOR TWO

Edith was the first to congratulate him. She looked at me with amazement when I opened the dressing room door, but at that moment I didn't pay too much attention. People's gestures of surprise – of fright, almost – on seeing me for the first time stopped being relevant to me some time ago. Many need to look up to meet my gaze. I must confess that this gave me a complex until I discovered the advantages of observing and defying people from above. For one thing, it's fun to realize how few of them dare provoke me. It's very unlikely that anyone will bother me on the street. But the best thing is that Father lets me take care of his violin. He says it's safer with me, that only a crazy person would attempt to take it away from me, and then he laughs. That's why when we travel he takes charge of all the rest of the luggage and I concentrate only on guarding the Stradivarius. I was just putting it away in its case when Father told me I could let in the audience members who wanted to see him. There was a long row of people, as always, but she was the first to enter.

Edith had seen several people drying their tears as they listened to Fabián play the violin. The orchestra musicians rose to their feet to applaud him for several minutes, and at people's insistence he gave two encores. As soon as he finished the second, Edith hurried to get to the dressing room, as they had agreed the prior afternoon. She wanted to tell him how much she'd enjoyed the concert and, besides, she was terribly curious to see Rebecca: the last time they were together, the girl was only five, although she looked older.

Fabián had spoken to her of his daughter with pride during the cancer fundraiser where they'd run into each other by chance. "She does sculptures in marble." Edith remembered Rebecca's pale face perfectly, her light-coloured eyes, her childlike voice that asked for her mother when Fabián still didn't know how to explain to her that she was dead.

"Marble? She's that strong?" she asked right away.

Fabián nodded.

"Wait till you see her."

Edith found it almost impossible to imagine what Rebecca would be like now, how she would behave, and that made her somewhat nervous as she waited outside the door.

People had formed a long line, readying their pens and programs. Several minutes later the door was opened, and Edith had to try hard to hide her astonishment upon seeing Rebecca. She realized immediately why her father had compared her to a Valkyrie.

Father greeted her with surprising familiarity, and it was at that instant that I recognized her. I almost never forget people's faces, though I must admit I didn't remember hers in detail. Then he introduced us.

"Becky, this is Edith. Do you remember her?"

"No, not at all. Why?"

Edith smiled at me and held out her hand. Shaking a clammy hand is so unpleasant for me that I automatically wiped mine on my skirt after the exchange. Edith was disconcerted, but luckily Father didn't catch on because he was busy with other people. She took advantage of the chance to explain to me that we already knew each other but that the last time she had seen me I was too little, so it would understandably be difficult for me to remember that now. I preferred not to make any comment about it.

"What a nice concert, don't you think?"

The poor woman was not very original, so I didn't even turn to look at her. I just sat down in the armchair, with the violin case on my lap, waiting for Father to finish.

Edith didn't know what to talk about with Rebecca, but she thought it wasn't good manners to keep quiet. She thought Fabián would blame her for not being friendly with his daughter, and it had been so long since she had seen them that she wanted to make a good impression.

"Do you play too?"

I hate to be asked that question.

"No. And you?"

Edith didn't understand why Rebecca looked at her with such disdain or why her attempts at being nice were backfiring. She looked at Fabián, who was conversing with some of the musicians in the orchestra, and hoped he would be done soon. Perhaps during dinner things would get better. She resolved to be patient and sat down beside Rebecca, who immediately went over to her father.

"Daddy, let's go. I'm hungry."

Father said goodbye to everyone except Edith. I realized then that she would be coming with us to the restaurant. After concerts, both in our hometown and abroad, we always went out to eat with some friends, musicians from the orchestra and acquaintances. This time it would be just us and Edith. I forced a smile so that Father couldn't accuse me of being impolite. I thought it would just be a matter of pretending for a few hours, so I resigned myself to it. Would we be going to the usual place Father liked when we were *home, or somewhere new? I was curious but didn't ask, so that Edith wouldn't think I cared too much about it.*

To my surprise, however, we didn't go to a restaurant. Father told Ambrose, our chauffeur, to drive us to our place. "What do you mean our place? We have to go somewhere else to celebrate," I insisted. He smiled and stroked my hair. "No. I'd rather be somewhere peaceful," he replied. I couldn't see Edith's face because I was looking out the window at the street, but I could swear she smiled. If she knew Father, she must have known that he almost never invited guests home.

It was better to look out at the street than at Fabián, with his daughter's hand between his as she insisted on going to a restaurant. Dining at Fabián's house, seeing the place he lived in now, made her happy, and Rebecca's anger – she had to confess – made her feel important. She felt she really couldn't complain, and so she kept quiet.

"You don't know this, but Edith was about to become your mother."

"Will you pass me the bread, Daddy?"

Yes, I did know it. And it was clear she still wanted to be, but I simply preferred not to hear any more about the matter. I took a roll, broke it into several pieces and played with the crumbs during most of the dinner. I couldn't eat a bite.

Edith blushed.

She recalled Fabián's rejection to her offer to be together all too well. "Rebecca doesn't accept anyone being in her mother's place. You have to understand that." Edith understood and therefore decided to stop seeing him. But this time she wasn't willing to give in so easily.

"So you ran into each other at the fundraiser the other day. What a coincidence."

"That's right."

She didn't fool me. She must have known that Father was going to be playing to help raise funds for cancer research and she went there to see him. But she wasn't going to get away with it.

When Rebecca agreed to show her the house, Edith felt relieved, almost contented. At the back of a very large garden was Becky's sculpture workshop, a spacious room with several windows.

Scattered on the floor were sheets of newspaper, tools and several small blocks of marble. Atop the table was one which was larger than the rest, half finished.

"Who is it?"

"Euterpe."

She didn't know what I was talking about.

"The Greek Muse of music. I'm sculpting her for father."

I only needed to complete the detail on her face and arms. I wanted to have her finished so I could give her to father before we went to Berlin. It was only six weeks until his concert with the Philharmonic.

Besides the workshop, Rebecca showed her the gym, which was in an adjacent room. It had all been especially built for Rebecca, so she could have some privacy and work on her sculptures at peace while her father practiced the violin.

"I wouldn't know what to do with all this equipment," Edith said.

No, of course she wouldn't.

The workshop had an ensuite bathroom which was one of her favorite places, Rebecca told her: it was decorated with real plants, and had a huge skylight, a sauna, and an antique bathtub.

"How beautiful! It has legs and everything!"

I showed her the whole house, with the exception of Father's studio. It turned my stomach to think of her making some stupid remark about that sacred place. But Father took her there and told her the story behind some of the paintings and our photographs. He said there were no pictures of Mother because her memory was painful to both of us. So we preferred to display only our own, taken in England, Buenos Aires, Moscow. *But to me, Mother's memory was no longer painful. I guess that's because of how little I really knew her. I refused to put her photograph in the studio because it would have been a distraction for Father. He'd have another face to look at, besides mine, and that bothered me.*

Edith felt goosebumps when he agreed to play a piece for her on the violin. She didn't even turn to check Rebecca's reaction: she never took her eyes off Fabián for a moment.

That was too much. Paganini is my favourite. How could he dare play him for her?

"He's Becky's favourite composer. Ever since she was little I've been playing one or two pieces every night before she goes to sleep."

Well, at least he put away the violin before Edith had a chance to ask to see it up close. I was starting to feel more relieved until Father asked Edith to visit us again the next day. I made it a point to chime in: I told Father not to pressure her, that maybe she would be bored coming back to see us so soon, but she handled it well. How was she going to be bored with us if she liked us so much? I hated the gleam in her eye. That night I didn't want to listen to any more Paganini before bed, and naturally I didn't get any sleep.

I couldn't keep the two of them from going out several times together. While they were out I would shut myself up in my workshop to work on my sculpture, but I couldn't shape the muse's arms to my satisfaction. I couldn't decide what position they should be in. I was anxious about the trip to Berlin because I wanted to finish the statue on time, although deep down it was a consolation to know that the date was fast approaching and it would be the perfect opportunity to get away from Edith.

"What about school?"

"I quit a year ago."

Fabián explained that Rebecca had asked him for a few months' break, not just so they could be together for a longer time, but so that she could make a decision about her professional aspirations. If she definitely chose sculpture, he would want to spend all the time he could with her before sending her off to study. It would be hard to be apart, and he didn't want to pressure her. Edith agreed. She searched for some gesture on Rebecca's part that would signal the approval she expected to get in exchange, but she saw nothing out of the ordinary. Rebecca only paid attention to the actions and words of her father.

I was about to scream but managed to control myself. Father told me after he had been practicing the violin for several hours. It's true, there was something strange in the notes I happened to hear him play that morning. I don't know why I didn't pick up on it. He came into the workshop and told me: Edith would be coming to live with us.

How could he do that to me? To us? How could I concentrate on my sculpture now?

Edith didn't have much luggage, and she quickly found a place for her clothes next to Fabián's.

No. I couldn't concentrate on the sculpture; or on anything.

The trip to Berlin would be the ideal opportunity to spend more time with him. Besides, she was fed up with Rebecca's indifference and wanted to teach her a lesson.

"I promise you I'll do everything possible to win her over," she lied. "Let me go with you."

I broke it.

I broke the sculpture when I found out she'd be coming along on the trip. It was too much, too much for me to handle. Who did she think she was, creeping into my life like that? How could Father not see what she was trying to do?

Two days before leaving, Edith decided to give the house a thorough cleaning. She emptied the shelves in order to clean off Fabian's scores one by one, and she refused to let the servants help her. Rebecca sat sullenly in an armchair watching her. Then she went up to her room and stayed there the whole afternoon because, as Edith was cleaning the studio, Fabián had to lock himself up in Rebecca's workshop to practice his instrument. At nightfall, Edith went in to tell him that all the scores were back in place and that he could return to the house to continue playing. There would be no further interruptions.

"You look exhausted."

"Yes, I'm tired, but don't worry."

"Why don't you take a nice bath in Becky's tub? It's a good way to relax."

"What if she gets angry?"

"She won't. You'll find some clean towels there. Go on, it's the best bathroom in the house!"

"I'm embarrassed."

"Don't be silly. I'll be in the bedroom waiting for you."

When I saw Father cross the garden toward the house, I decided to come down and straighten up in my workshop. I had not planned to do any more sculptures until I got back from Berlin, but I did want to sit down and do a sketch, and the table was still covered with the remnants of the figure I had broken. I left my bedroom cautiously. I didn't want to run into Edith.

The sky was completely dark when Edith stretched out her legs and arms, allowing the water to surround her and cover her slowly. Steam began to fill the room gradually. At that instant she thought she had never before felt so much at peace, so satisfied. The wait had been worth it. And since the first day she had wondered what it would be like to be soaking in that tub.

I heard the noise of the water. In my bathroom. There was someone in my bathroom. It had to be her. How dare she?

As the water level rose in the tub, Edith imagined what her future would be like with Fabián. She would be always at his side, caring for him. Rebecca would just have to get used to it. Besides, perhaps it wouldn't be long before she wasn't an only child anymore: Edith had resolved to convince Fabián to have a baby.

What was she doing in my bathroom without my permission? And in my tub, nonetheless? This time I would have the nerve to tell her off, to say to her face what I really thought of her.

She stood up when she saw Rebecca enter, furious, almost running toward her. She tried to apologize to her and calm her down. But Rebecca was ranting uncontrollably. Edith thought her anger made her look bigger, stronger than ever, almost bestial. For the first time she was afraid of her and took a step backward in retreat.

And when she stepped out of the tub she slipped. I saw her fall on her back and strike her head against the edge of the tub. The blood seeped out and stained the mosaic tiles around the feet of the tub. I don't know how or when she hit her head. I didn't get a good look because I closed my eyes. At that instant, just at that instant the image I had been searching for appeared in my mind: the smiling face of Euterpe with her arms outstretched, as though she were waiting for someone.

My heart was pounding and my hands trembled. I thought immediately of going for help, telling Father about Edith, but first I had to run and sketch that silhouette on a sheet of paper so I wouldn't forget a single detail, so I could execute the sculpture when I returned from Berlin. To help me calm down a little and take my mind off what had just happened, I cleaned off the table and put the tiles in order. I realized that Edith's clumsiness couldn't be helped, it was what it was. And I wouldn't have time to do my work later, would I? The preparations for the trip, Edith's wake, and the funeral would be a source of worry for me, keeping me away from my workshop. And I wanted to finish my sculpture so I could give it to Father for his birthday at the latest.

Before returning to my bedroom, I went in to look at Edith. Luckily, her blood hadn't reached the wood of my sauna. Everything else could be easily cleaned with chlorine. It would all be back to normal soon.

I turned the lights off in my workshop before heading back to the house, but I left the light in my bathroom on, so as not to give rise to any suspicion. I knew it was only a matter of time before someone would find her. In hindsight, it was a fortunate accident. Father couldn't blame me for anything, and the best part was that from then on, when he played his violin in the evenings, it would be for me. For me only.

ANTS

I had insomnia and spent the whole night killing ants.

Since early summer, when Tomás died, they've taken over the house. One long row of little black specks moving along the wall, scurrying back and forth from the window to the kitchen table. They've invaded the bathroom, my closet and the cupboard, too, even though it's empty. Some of them were speeding nervously along the tabletop, as though they figured the freedom I had unwillingly granted them would be short-lived and they wanted to enjoy the remnants of the feast of sugared wax and ground cocoa. Others, who had reconnoitered the rest of the rooms more thoroughly, decided to set up camp in the drawer where El Flaco is. I don't like to look at them, so I never go near there.

When I first decided to go on a diet, we'd hidden some cookies on the shelves of the armoire, underneath the mattress, even inside the old tape recorder with no batteries. It was Tomás's idea: at some point, when I was unable to cope with my hunger, they might be a help. Then he got sick and died, and I forgot about them. They must be spoiled by now, but the ants like them anyway. They walk onto them, eat their fill from the tops of the cookies, then haul the crumbs off to some place outside the window. I haven't discovered their anthill, but I know it's there in the yard, maybe near Isabel's rusty swing. The grass has grown high and uneven and it's covered with dry leaves, because autumn arrived a few days after I made up my mind not to leave the house, and I haven't swept or raked since then.

In case Isabel might come back, I'd always set three places at the table. Tomás never resigned himself to her being away, and he was insistent that everything should be impeccable to greet her when she returned. It was out of the question to get rid of the swing or any of her other things: her photographs, books, the doll with the matted hair, and her clothes all remained exactly where she had left them. Right after Tomás died I tried to keep up the routine, but setting two places instead of three and seeing that every afternoon one of them was left undisturbed began to depress me, so I stopped doing it. Now it seems useless and stupid to clean a place where I'm the only one, and I don't even sit down at the table to eat any more. Until recently I only used the table to prepare the candles, but the sugar ran out, I ate the cocoa, and everything else is full of ants, so there's no way I can continue casting the spell.

Besides, after today it won't matter.

I began doing it in secret, a few days before Tomás died, to see if I could get Isabel to come back home. I knew how important it was for him to see her again; that's why I did it. I went and bought several packages of tallow candles, and with a wooden toothpick I'd write the names of Tomás and Isabel on them one by one, over and over, in tiny letters, until they were completely covered. Then I'd coat them with the sugar and cocoa mixture and light them while reciting the Lord's Prayer. At first I did just one every night, so that Tomás wouldn't notice, but when he took a turn for the worse and couldn't leave his room, I'd fix up two or three and leave them burning until dawn.

I sent Isabel several emails, but she didn't answer. "Maybe she's taking a trip," I told Tomás when he asked about her again, although I knew for a fact it wasn't true. I knew she was in the city and she didn't come home because she still hadn't forgiven me. The smell of smoke and medicine soon filled the house, particularly after I closed up all the windows to keep out the draft. The odour got worse because of El Flaco, but by now I'm used to that, too. The ants were able to get in through a tiny hole in the sill; a spider wove her web a little higher up, near the crank. Until yesterday, the spider was the only one concerned with the ants.

The last few nights of Tomás's agony were the hardest. I would have felt abandoned if it hadn't been for the arrival of El Flaco, a scrawny, flea-bitten cat who, after one can of tuna, turned into *my* cat and was constantly at my side, as I'd give Tomás a sponge bath or feed him while I cleaned house or prepared the candles. Tomás spurned the animal, but he was too weak to protest when El Flaco began roaming freely about the house. No, I hadn't forgotten that Isabel was allergic, but I wasn't going to banish the cat solely on that account. I promised Tomás that if Isabel came back I'd keep the cat in the yard.

It wasn't necessary. El Flaco left on his own when I no longer had anything to feed him. I left him on the street before I shut myself in. It was only two - maybe three - weeks ago that he came back, but at first I refused to let him in. He just stayed there, meowing and meowing, and I stood behind the door with a knot in my throat, because how could I explain things to him? A lady rang the doorbell one morning to let me know that "my cat was outside and wanted in." I told her he wasn't mine and she could take him if she wanted. Then I changed my mind and opened the door. El Flaco looked pretty sick, so I picked him up, took him to my room and kept petting him until sleep overcame me. The next morning he was stiff and cold. I couldn't endure the idea of burying him; he didn't deserve it. I wrapped him up in a plastic bag and put him in a drawer.

I think he was so inconsiderate that he only came back to me in order to die. As if I hadn't suffered enough with the death of Tomás.

Isabel didn't come to the wake or the funeral. I telephoned her several times, but she'd hang up as soon as she recognized my voice. I left messages on her answering machine but to no avail. Just because I had so many left over, I kept on with the candles, praying for her to return so that we could talk. The last candle burned out the day after El Flaco died, when I had already given up hope. I didn't think it had worked. But I was wrong.

Isabel came to see me yesterday afternoon.

I wasn't going to let her in. I should have refused. Tomás wasn't there to stop me, and honestly, at that point I was the one who wasn't willing to forgive her for abandoning us like that. For shutting us out. For not loving me back. Even so, I finally went and opened the door. She had a point: the house belonged to both of us. But she had gone away and I stayed. She lost her rights to the place and to Tomás, although she was always his darling little girl. *Our* darling little girl.

Isabel was quite surprised when she saw me. "You look thin, *very* thin," she emphasized. And dirty – of course, because I haven't paid the water bill, which she didn't actually say, but I know she thought it. But I don't have any gas either and I hate to take a bath with cold water. And naturally I was going to be thin, because I had just finished my diet when Tomás died, and after that the food we had in the house started to run out.

When she looked out the kitchen window and compared the yard to a jungle I couldn't say anything. Time, I guess, had just been doing its thing all along.

Then she suddenly bent over the kitchen sink and vomited; I suppose the odour got to her. I thought of telling her about El Flaco, but she would have taken it wrong. Then I realized she was aghast at all the ants, and it was only then that I noticed how many there really were.

How many there really are.

She started the argument. She didn't have to lie: if she'd really been worried about Tomás and me, she would have come sooner. "I couldn't bear the thought of seeing you," she told me. "You make me sick." Then I asked her why she'd never really made a clean break from Tomás and me. Why she kept in touch, randomly phoned Tomás to check on him, and altogether made us believe that she'd drop in unexpectedly some afternoon. I stood there in front of her, looking right at her, but she couldn't withstand the intensity of my gaze. Now she was the one who didn't know how to respond.

Coward.

Tomás was all I had. I loved feeling his caresses, the way his hands and his lips moved along my breasts. Isabel was always there with us. It was impossible to hide from her. I always told her I wasn't trying to take her mother's place or steal her father away from her. The proof of that was the fact that the best nights were the ones all three of us spent together. Isabel's sweet scent mixed with the odour of tobacco from Tomás's pipe. Her tender skin was so soft that he and I would have wanted to caress it forever. With our hands, our tongues. But then she grew up and began to refuse our company. She was becoming a beautiful young lady, and she didn't want us to touch her anymore. She wouldn't even let us bathe her the way we used to, taking turns to wash her soft skin and run our hands over her tender body. She'd shut herself up in her room and not come out. We tried to force her into submission, until it became impossible to hold on to her.

This isn't – wasn't – the first time she tells – told – me that I make her sick.

"If you forgive me, I'll forgive you too," I said, although I wasn't entirely convinced that I meant it. Her rejecting our unique kind of love would be hard to forgive; her not coming home to see Tomás before he died was unforgivable. But I owed Tomás to give it an honest try. I tried to stroke her hair and touch her face. It had been so long since I'd seen her that I'd forgotten the way her skin smelled. But she pulled away. She was leaning on the stove and walked over toward the wall opposite the window, as though trying to get away from the ants as well. That hurt me deeply.

She had no reason to look down on me like that.

Not after I had waited for her for so many days, with her place set at the table and the house all clean.

But I couldn't tell her that, because when I tried to approach her again she felt cornered and threatened me with a butcher knife. The drawer was broken, and the utensils were spread out all over the counter. She said there was nothing she needed to be forgiven for, that it was the other way around. I laughed at her, at her fearful little eyes and that absurd knife in her hand. I knew she wouldn't hurt me; she had hardly changed at all since the last time we saw each other. I thought she wanted to play, like when she was a little girl and she'd beg me to chase her around the yard. This time the door was shut, and she couldn't run away.

I went up to her slowly, and finally she lowered the knife.

No sooner had I stretched out my arms to put them around her shoulders than she raised the knife again to attack me. The sudden look of determination I discovered in her eyes unnerved me, but feeling the knife blade graze my hand prompted me to react. We struggled. I don't know where I found the strength to defend myself. Then I felt her body shrink back and, almost at the same instant, something warm soaking my blouse. Before I could hold her head up she fell to the floor. It took me a few seconds to understand what had occurred.

What I still can't comprehend is how it all happened.

She, too, had come back to me in order to die.

I wiped the blood off her hands and abdomen with the sheets from Tomás's bed, so she could feel something of his. He would have liked that. Now my fingers are red, too. I tried to lick them clean but it's useless. Saliva doesn't dissolve blood after it's had a chance to dry.

I'm thirsty and afraid, but most of all I'm very sleepy.

All night long I was killing ants.

Deeper and deeper inside Isabel.

R IS FOR RADISHES
ON REMEMBRANCE DAY

It's still dark when I enter the kitchen in the early morning to check on the radishes. I've never planted anything before; I'm nervous and eager to see what I'll find nesting in the moist soil – I feel like a little girl about to unearth a treasure. The leaves are bright green and look almost happy, as if they, too, had been waiting for today. Not a sound can be heard. Gabby is still sleeping and I know I have to wait for her to wake up before exploring the contents of the ceramic pot that has been sitting on our windowsill for twenty-five days now. Outside, the hushed wind seems to pay its respects to my memories. In my mind, I hear Galina's strong voice declaring the radish a most loyal vegetable, because every part of it can be eaten and it's easy to plant and care for. Her smile was yellow and nonchalant. I'm wearing her favourite pink robe and suddenly wish I had some of the lilac perfume she used to wear, to feel her even closer.

It's been eleven years since we were last together in this same place. I wanted to do something special to say goodbye. To part with her in a happier mood, and feel less guilty about letting go. No. Letting go is a euphemism. I was betraying her and even though everybody said I was exaggerating and she wouldn't know she was being moved into an old-age home, it was enough that *I* knew it. Her getting out of the house unnoticed and wandering alone around the city for an entire day, in the cold, asking for directions to get to her childhood home – striving to arrive at an apartment that had been long gone, on the other side of the world – finally did it for me. Remembering the fear that gnawed at me during those merciless hours trying to find her still makes me shiver. The police reports, the driving around the neighbourhood screaming her name, the making of flyers in a flash to hand out to anyone who would take one made me realize how blind I had been. I couldn't take care of her on my own any longer, especially when I was about to become a single mother. Only a few days later did it dawn on me that our last afternoon together happened to be on November 11.

For weeks now have I been trying to decide how to share the story with Gabby. What will she say when she sees me dressed like this? At what point should I tell her about Galina's notebook? A shy ray of light is starting to crawl through the window. It will be a partly cloudy day. Perfect to fit my mood.

As my Galina – she never wanted me to call her Grandma, complaining it made her feel old – began to fade away, I made an effort to claw her back from oblivion. To keep her with me for as long as I could. So I began doing the things we always used to share together: baking cookies, going out for walks to familiar places, reading stories. I reminded her again and again of the time she gave me a "pooch of honour" for being brave at the hospital when my appendix was removed. I smile and look at it now, still sitting proudly on top of the microwave table – it's a stuffed toy in the shape of a lamb but she called it *pooch*, with a strong *p*. Everything about her had always seemed strong and everlasting, and that's what made it so hard to witness the frustration in her eyes and her half-open mouth as she tried to reach inside herself to retrieve words and memories that were eroding. Even her body seemed to shrink as she forgot how to sit and walk straight. I didn't understand how small she had really become until she started mistaking me for her little sister, Agnieszka, who hadn't survived the war. It was then I remembered a story Galina had told me once, about how during her last summer at home with her mother and sister – they never saw my great-grandfather again after he joined the army a year before – they had tried to rekindle a feel for happiness.

When war was declared between Germany and Russia, and the sirens in Warsaw started to howl more often than ever before, Agnieszka suffered panic attacks. It was very hard for Galina and her mother to take her down to the shelter because she would freeze and refuse to move. As the Russian flyers began to circle around Warsaw, the sound of bombs made the air tremble. There was no way they could even think about happy times then, and Agnieszka's health was deteriorating quickly. So one day, after they emerged from the basement, Galina came up with an idea.

"Let's wear these." She had their swimming suits in her hand. "It's very warm right now, and I'm sure these suits will make us feel better."

Agnieszka and her mother hesitated, but the moment they held those suits in their hands, they smiled – and Galina's amber eyes beamed as she shared the memory with me. There remains only one photo of Agnieszka and it's the image I recall whenever I think of her: a scrawny preteen with long, braided hair, a vivacious gaze and a nose just like mine.

Galina was very excited to be out of her regular, worn clothes and have her bathing suit on, but she had lost so much weight that it was too big for her. She would have cried if she had seen herself in the mirror, but instead she went to the living room and hung an old sheet close by the window, under the sun. She laid another sheet on the floor, and sat down to wait for her mother and little sister.

"We are having a window-side party," she declared as they came in, clothed in their way-too-big suits. None complained or made fun of the other. They lay there, letting the sun warm their bodies, eating radishes they had grown in their kitchen.

Later, in July, there was a typhus epidemic, and people became sick with dysentery and pleurisy. Mother asked them to stay indoors. Agnieszka and Galina, to console themselves, wore their bathing suits and sat down under the sun that came through the window. They sat reading, their shoes and dresses and a first-aid kit ready in case a siren howled. Agnieszka still cried but at least she had stopped refusing to follow Galina and their mother to the building's basement.

By the end of September, Kiev had fallen and London was under severe bombardment by the Nazis. Shots were often heard on the street. It was risky to go outside. Their window-side parties were over. It was safer to live with the curtains closed. Galina said: "I don't know if Mama noticed this, but Agnieszka still wore her bathing suit under her regular clothes. She was holding onto something that could make her happy, my little sister."

That is why, on our last afternoon together, I turned up the heating and helped Galina sit down in a chair by the living-room window. I sat on the floor on a spread sheet. It was a sunny afternoon and Galina was quiet and all I could hear was the crunching of radishes and her soft breathing. I was about to be lost in sadness, but just when I thought Galina had forgotten how to remember that last summer with her family, and as I fought to hold back my tears, Galina took me by surprise:

"I hope you never have to live through a war, ever, my darling," she said, her hand reaching out to caress my hair, her hand bony and raddled by liver spots, and yet so beautiful. I was about to say something, but she hushed me and went on: "Little Agnieszka looked like a fairy in her swimming suit. It was blue, did I tell you that? It matched her eyes." She fixed her gaze on my swollen stomach, and blew it a kiss. I moved closer to her pale, venous legs and let my head rest against her knee. We stayed like that for a few minutes. I felt so sheltered sitting there, her hand resting on my head. For a moment, I thought it would all be okay, it would all be back to the way it was. But when I lifted my head to look at her, her gaze was lost again. I rose to my feet and tried to make her speak, to make her recognize me, but it was useless.

Galina never returned to Warsaw after the war. She never told me why, never wanted to share those details with me, but I discovered the reason when I was leafing through an old notebook of hers after she passed away. I didn't want to do something she would have disapproved of, but found it so hard not to read it. So I allowed myself a random paragraph. Galina's words surprised me, because my eyes landed on the one that seemed to answer most of my questions.

I can't fight the tears as I sit down with her notebook and reread her words in this crisp, early morning light. I've decided that Galina's notebook will be Gabby's. One day, she will be mature enough. My Galina will not be forgotten and I'll still have respected her privacy the way she wanted me to. For now, however, I take advantage of the peace around me as I ache for her soft touch.

I heard a troop of German soldiers coming close to where I had been searching for Agnieszka and Mama. I immediately looked for a place to hide. I entered a building and went into an open apartment. There were so many abandoned apartments then, all looted by Polish and German thieves. Most of the first apartments that had been vacated belonged to Jewish families, because they were forced to move into the Ghetto. We got used to that happening and even began seeing it as a normal procedure. And now we were in the same situation. Even though my own apartment looked now abandoned, too, it somehow took me by surprise to find so many others desolated in the exact same way. I could make out silhouettes on the walls, the marks left behind by furniture and paintings. And I got this idea that, somewhere inside the walls, the lost voices of the people who had once lived and laughed there were still trapped, wondering what had happened, why everything had gone so wrong. All of a sudden I knew it: while I had been waiting in vain for Mama and Agnieszka to return home, I had searched for their voices inside our apartment, trapped inside the walls. That explained my urge to lean against them, to caress them the way I had caressed Agnieszka's hair at night when she crawled into bed with me. Those walls had seen us grow up. And they had seen my family be taken away. Somewhere inside them, their last words had found a nest.

With Warsaw's destruction, the voices that for centuries had been asleep between the walls of the old buildings and houses, the voices of the people who had lived and died in Warsaw's dwellings, were left homeless. I imagined they became blind, invisible butterflies floating above the rubble. They had nowhere to go. None of them would ever rest again. They had nowhere to go back to. And it was then that I knew there was no going back for me, either.

The thing is, in the end her mind played a trick on her and she did try to go back and, in doing so, she hastened our parting. After our last afternoon together, Galina did not come back to me either. I visited her every other day but the light inside her eyes was ever-dimming. She disintegrated slowly and there was nothing I could do to stop it – only Gabby's kicks and hiccups inside me kept me going, a constant reminder that not even the most magnificent of miracles comes to us free.

No matter how much time goes by, I still feel a need to return to Galina, and have chosen to do so every November 11. Today will be the first time that I will have let Gabby into my little tradition – my precious girl, whose slumber steps are now filling the hallway and coming close to me. As I turn to welcome her into the kitchen and into our past, I can't help but laugh when she asks, her mouth suddenly wide open:

"Why on earth are you wearing a swimming suit?"

I need to blow my nose, to dry my eyes; most of all, I need to hug her – but before I go to Gabby, I hide Galina's notebook behind my *pooch of honour*. It will be safe there for a few hours, until I can put it back into its drawer. I embrace my surprised daughter – my plump, tall and healthy daughter – the sweet scent of shampoo still lingering in her hair, and I know that we are blessed. Holding her tight, I whisper:

"Remember the seeds we planted a couple of weeks ago?"

THE LAST CONFESSION

My name is Marcela, but I'm still startled when someone calls out the name "Maria." I shiver, I have this urge to run away as fast as I can... My heart beats, my hands sweat... It's absurd, especially in the middle of winter. Here, freezing wind is the only enemy. It hurts to breathe, but I know there are worse things. The wind reminds me I am in Toronto and, no matter how much I miss the warmth of the sun all year round, and the mangoes that grow in the tree in my mother's backyard, I'm safe. But for how long? I had just come out of the shower this morning when I turned on the radio and heard the news. The government back home has been overthrown. Political prisoners are being freed. Trials will be held. I had dreamed about this moment – how I'd react, what I might say. In spite of it all, I had envisioned receiving the news while in the company of my loved ones, never alone like this. I had expected to feel overjoyed. But I peed in my underwear. After cleaning myself, I didn't know what else to do, so I phoned Farah.

"Congratulations! You must be elated!" she said as soon as she recognized my voice.

I took a deep breath. It was hard to find air to push the words out.

"Can I see you, please? I need to talk."

"What about the snowstorm? They say it will be big this time."

This Canadian habit, this talking about the weather all the time, drives me crazy. Farah, of all people, should know there are more urgent, grave matters to worry about.

"The forecast people always exaggerate. Please, Farah. I'm begging you."

She agreed to meet me at the café close to her apartment building. I have time to get everything ready. The bed is unmade, the bookshelf is half-empty, and I still have yesterday's coffee ageing on the stove. I take a piece of paper, a pen I brought home from work and sit down, close my eyes and see Tomás's face, his fat-framed glasses, and the freckles on his nose. He was very serious and committed, but also had the most contagious laughter. I write down *Tomás*, and a knot takes my throat hostage. I need a few moments to be able to breathe again, to focus again, and write down his last name. I can't go on. I have to stop. I get up and walk toward the window. I hesitate before lifting the corner of the curtain to look outside. My knees are trembling, but my back is covered in sweat, so I know it's not the old heater's fault this time.

Maybe I should have chosen a different name, but Maria seemed just right: back then I, too, was a virgin. The control I had over my body made me feel strong. Maria was the name I used for our work underground. I thought I would be protected by its profound religious meaning, but also because it is such a common name. I was wrong. When they arrested me they knew exactly who I was. They knew Marcela, and they knew Maria, and nothing could save me.

This is my second winter in Toronto. I tell myself I like winter because it helps me to stay focused on the present. I peek out under the curtain and see the sky is white. I can't make out a single cloud. I hope the storm is a tough one. The sun that smiled at me from the blue sky during the summer was an injection of melancholy: I got homesick. That's why I have been doing the opposite of what everybody else normally does around here: I go out and take long walks when it is grey and snowing, but when it is hot I try to stay indoors as much as I can. In the beginning I left the curtains and the windows shut, but memories of the time when I didn't know whether it was day or night, or if it had rained, were too strong. I opted to stay indoors, curtains closed but windows wide open. The breeze pushed sunshine my way; allowing the light back in was a little victory. I live on the sixth floor. Nobody was spying on me from the outside. I kept reminding myself that this was Toronto, but the heat and the humidity somehow fooled me. I couldn't stop thinking of my last days back home. During winter I'm more at ease. When it's snowing I don't have to be so vigilant. The scarf over my face helps me feel protected. The crispy – or slushy - sounds beneath my boots let me know if I am alone. I know immediately when someone is behind me; I seek refuge against a wall and let the person – or persons – pass, and then keep walking.

I met Farah at work. We are telemarketers. It's not a nice job, but it is the only one I could get as a newcomer, and it helps me pay my rent and food. I walk to the office, sit down at my little desk, and tackle faceless names and numbers they assign to me. I call the customers and read my script to them, and most of the time they hang up on me or insult me or yell at me. How dare I interrupt their meal or their work or their privacy or whatever. At the beginning I couldn't sell anything, so one morning my boss threatened to fire me, which then turned out to be a blessing because that's how Farah and I became friends. I was crying in the washroom during one of our breaks. She offered me some advice. She gave me a hug! Nobody had touched me since I'd left home. I just broke down when I felt her warmth, her smell of saffron and sandalwood. I hugged her back and thought I would never be able to stop crying. She later joked that I had made her *chador* all wet, and I asked her what a *chador* was, and when she told me we both smiled.

Our office is a small place, yet everyone comes from a different country (none from mine, though, and nobody speaks Spanish except me). If somebody took a picture of my co-workers and myself together and sent it back home, my cousins would laugh and say we look like one of those old ads that *Benetton* posted everywhere in the eighties. Yes, in my country we were never rich but we were trendy and aware of the latest fashions, even if the faces on the poster didn't resemble our daily world. Ours is a homogenous society, that's why we were so easy to catch, so easy to brainwash. But I like to fantasize: with such a picture in my hand, I would tell my family something like this: "*Sí*, in Toronto I don't even know where in the map to find the country where this co-worker here comes from, but that's okay because we smile at one another every morning and sometimes we share food, and it's a great feeling, *sabes?*" My cousin Pedro would have known what I mean. Not only would he have understood, he'd have wanted to come and see for himself. Maybe even try to hook up with some girl whose name he would have fun mispronouncing... *Ay, Pedro*, I miss you so much. If we only knew where your body is, what they did to you... Aunt Clara has probably worn herself out by now looking for him, trying to find anything out. Her hair had already turned grey when they arrested me, and she was not even fifty. If only I was brave enough to speak with her again...

I'm happy – if you can ever be happy about things like these – that my mom wasn't alive when they took me. I couldn't have handled the thought of them doing something to her because of me. I couldn't have handled the thought of her crying because of my choices. And if somebody had ever told me that the only person who would have understood me was the woman underneath the black veil, I wouldn't have believed it. But now I live in Toronto, and since I take walks at thirty degrees below zero, anything is possible.

Farah, a few years older than me, has the most beautiful dark hair. I saw it when she took off her veil – we were alone – to show me her biggest scar. In both our countries, anyone who is against the regime gets killed. Or imprisoned and tortured, at least in mine.

Until this morning.

Farah and I have a lot in common: we know what pain and fear taste like, the flavour and texture of our blood. We both have lost everything and everyone. Other people's cries are like tattoos inside my skull. Shrill, deep, under a tsunami of loud salsa music. I have nightmares almost every night: I deserve them. That's why I won't ever be able to face Aunt Clara and my cousins again. That's why I'm glad my mother passed away before all this happened.

I need to go back to the letters, back to writing the list, but it's so hard. It's much nicer to just stand here by the window. The streets are almost empty, which is strange considering it's Saturday and the storm is scheduled to begin later this afternoon. I can't help smiling when I see someone walking their dog and the dog is all dressed up. If Aunt Clara had heard about dogs wearing boots, she would have laughed until her jaws hurt. Some dogs' boots are nicer and cozier than mine. Farah thinks it's funny, too. She belongs to a group of survivors and refugees who get together every once in a while to comfort one another. She has asked me to come along, but I don't know if I can do that. I don't know if I can endure listening to their stories. And I would be so scared to find someone from my homeland. What would I say then? What excuse could I give? How could I ever look them in the eye? With Farah it's different. We can laugh at dogs wearing matching boots and coats, and if we feel like it, we can also talk, but mostly we don't anymore, and that's fine. She doesn't know my entire truth. Nobody does. The moment my words have a sound of their own and leave my body they will be impossible to take back. And I'm scared to confront them. In English there is a word or a name for almost everything. *Refugee* and *PTSD* are some of the first I learned. When they are said out loud, people seem to understand, they turn benevolent and generous. Nothing wrong with that, but what do they really understand, I wonder. Unlike me, most of them do know where their loved ones have been laid to rest. There is another convenient word to go with this, too, which I was taught upon arrival: closure. What an unbearable, cruel word. A pain so big can't be closed down.

Many times I've wondered about what Aunt Clara would say if I told her that people in Toronto actually *live* in basements. And that, when I refused to rent one, all I had to say was, "I'm a refugee and have been diagnosed with PTSD, so I can't live in a basement, thank you." Very polite, very politically correct. I am a fast learner. Nobody needs to know what happened – or if anything happened at all. Aunt Clara would have understood, though. She, too, would have rejected the basement apartment.

I got sick at work once. There was a mouse underneath one of the desks, a little brown mouse. I screamed so loudly I scared everyone. I ran to the washroom and locked myself in. I felt like my heart was about to break free from my chest. I threw up all over my clothes and was practically out of breath when the paramedics arrived. There's a name for that, too: *panic attack*. Farah looked me in the eye, she knew there were no words to describe what had driven me to the washroom. "Whenever you're ready," she'd said, "I'll be there." Hence today's call, the letters and the list. I will take her at her word. Our English is equally awkward, but I have learned since I arrived in Toronto that all languages become the same when spoken through sorrow.

I go back to the table and write *Rosa*. A chubby girl, with curly hair and incredibly white teeth; an only child. She lived with her dad, an old-fashioned man who wanted her to get married and have many children. She'd have none of that, Rosa... In English there are so many names and words for everything, but back home and in those days we used mostly one: *mierda*. Instead of saying, "The regime is corrupt," we would say, "El régimen es una mierda." Instead of saying, "We need to solve this problem," we said "Debemos resolver esta mierda." And of course, instead of saying someone had been "traumatized," we said "lo hicieron mierda;" they had turned him to shit.

And so, as I work down the list, and begin to write the letters, with every word I shape I tremble, I fight the urge to cry. I must not cry. By the time I'm finished I know I have to leave to meet Farah. It's so hard, however, to get up, put on my coat and my scarf and mittens and boots. I feel weak, scared; what if I don't go? I can call her and cancel. The storm would be a good excuse, she'd understand. But when I look at the envelopes I have in my hand, I know I must go. I don't want to bundle up, though. A sweater should do. I fold the documents, put them in my pocket, take my keys and leave without looking back.

The cold is numbing, yet, on this frigid noon as I walk through the snow, I feel surprisingly alert. I give myself strength by remembering Farah's laughter when I told her how Pedro and I would climb the mango tree in my mother's backyard and make a mess of our clothes eating all the mangoes, sitting there on a branch, and how my mother and Aunt Clara smiled at us and said we were the most beautiful monkeys they had ever seen. She had similar stories from back home, near the Caspian Sea, but they used to eat dates over there. So one day she brought in dates and I brought in some sliced mangoes and we shared our lunch quietly; we never did that again because we felt so sad. We decided tuna sandwiches are easier to share – no memories for either of us. Aunt Clara would have said we were silly girls, and perhaps she would have been right. What will she think when she learns that in this woman, from another faith, another language and another part of the world, I have found not just my only friend but the solution to my plight? Maybe getting to know her was why destiny brought me to live here.

January is a good time for new beginnings. Back home it's summer, and history is being written, as they said on the radio. Except I don't think they know, those Canadian radio hosts, that history is usually not written down in my country without first being beaten into the people. I wonder what is truly going on, but don't really want to find out. As I approach the café where I am to meet Farah, I think of Aunt Clara. She used to say that hope and calm always come together. I think she must have been wrong, because even though I have found hope, I am not calm. I'm shivering and my teeth are chattering and some people stare at me like I come from another planet. One woman even offers me her scarf. Why would I want a stranger's scarf? What difference would it make?

As I walk, I can't help but think of how I put my story into words for Farah to read. I cannot fight anymore and begin to cry, and the cold air mocks me and threatens to freeze my eyes but I don't care.

There were five of them around me, soldiers, laughing. They were new, I had never heard their voices before. I was tied up to the smelly, sticky operating table where they used to bring us in for questioning. The whole room stank of blood and sweat and mould. It was humid and cold and echoey, like basements usually are. The soldiers stank of cheap cologne. I always felt the urge to vomit when they brought me in, but how many times can you vomit on an empty stomach? I was expecting an electric shock, a beating, or being raped again. I never knew what would come first, my entire body was on alert. All of a sudden I felt something cool and heavy on my stomach. They informed me it was a small, metal cage. I heard a slight screech and then felt some cool paws and tiny claws scratching my skin. What is this, I asked, not daring to move. They removed my blindfold and the light hurt my eyes. After a few moments, I saw it: a big, black rat on top of my naked chest. It was sniffling, exploring me. I tried not to breathe. I didn't want it to bite me. The soldiers laughed and put minced meat on my breast, just a handful. It felt cold and wet. One of the soldiers said that the rat hadn't had anything to eat for days. My body was shaking against my will, and even though I was holding my lips closed tight I must have scared the rat because I felt its teeth pinching my skin. I started to scream and squirm. The rat scratched me before falling on the floor. The men were pissed off. They had to catch the rat again and they didn't like that, so one of them hit me while another put the blindfold back on. Once they caught the rat one of them said he felt like masturbating: it was a pity the rat was going to have me, and not him. "You can squirm all you want, cunt, but this little rodent wants his mamma." I was crying, pleading for mercy – please, let me go, please, I'll do anything, please. Another said it would be worse once they forced the animal inside my body. "Rats get scared and sometimes they get trapped in the uterus, then there's nothing we can do." I felt someone's fingers inside my vagina: "Yes, there's room enough here for that little critter for sure!" I couldn't handle it, I yelled and I promised I would tell them everything they wanted to know. All the names I knew, all the aliases, everything. Yes, we had a plan to kill the *Generalísimo*. Yes, there were many of us involved. "My breast hurts" was followed by, "Your cunt will hurt more!" and when I was done talking they punched me in the stomach, "You traitor, you make us sick!" they said, and gave me an electric shock. "Because you deserve it, you coward, you piece of rat shit."

When I woke up, I wasn't in my cell but in a convent. I have no idea how I got there. And will probably never know how or why either. I didn't ask questions, and neither did the nuns. I know it sounds strange, Farah, but it's true: they helped me get out of the country and start a new life. How involved with the regime were they? Who knows? Thanks to them and the good people in a Toronto parish, where I only went to Mass once, I came to this land of new beginnings and second chances. I don't think God exists. If he did, he wouldn't have created rats, or people who are willing to put rats up a woman's vagina, or people like me, who rat out their friends and family. No, I didn't want to call anyone, or see anyone before leaving. How could I? Forgive me, my dear Pedro. I was no match for you. Forgive me, Aunt Clara; I caused you more suffering when you already had enough. And please do forgive me, *mami*, for bringing such shame to our family. Tomás, Rosa, Liliana, Ismael, José, Blanca; Tomás, Rosa, Liliana, Ismael, José, Blanca; forgive me for what it is they did to you because of me. I say your names over and over again: they are my litany, almost a prayer. Only those whose names have been spoken can exist.

I'm crying so hard when I come to the café that I can't say anything to Farah. I just reach for the envelopes in my pocket, and give them to her. She wants to hug me, is shocked, tries to hold me back but I don't let her. People are staring. Who cares? I need to leave. If I'm numb enough from the cold it won't hurt. It will be brief. Fast. I run until she can't see me anymore. Tomás, Rosa, Liliana, Ismael, José, Blanca. It hurts to breathe even more than before. I force your names out into the icy-cold air – I can't run anymore, I'm so tired. I have the packages of powder from the hardware store in my pocket, the warfarin. I know what I must do, how I will finally break us all free. Saying my name over and over again: Marcela, Marcela, Marcela. My prayer, before I became Maria.

ACKNOWLEDGEMENTS

First of all, I would like to thank Barry Callaghan for opening Exile's door once again for me, and for his careful edits of my manuscript. The revision process was a wonderful learning experience for me. Barry, I'll be forever grateful for your patience and generosity.

They say it takes a village to raise a child, but I also know it to be true that it takes a village to have a manuscript ready for print. And before this book landed on Barry's desk I received very helpful feedback from several dear friends without whom I would have been lost. Debra Bennett, my dear amiga, thanks for staying up so many evenings reading through the early versions of my stories and offering kind and generous advice. Christina Kilbourne, I don't know what I would have done without your support in shaping the story that gives this book its title, thank you so much!

Gillian Bartlett, you hold a very special, unique place in my life, and in my writing. As my Fairy Godmother you have guided my hand with such patience, and have taught me so much, that I know I'll never be able to repay you. I love you. Thanks from the bottom of my heart.

Nina Callaghan, thank you so much for your careful revision of my manuscript in its last stage. You are a brilliant reader and your comments, questions and suggestions were enlightening and truly helpful.

Michael Callaghan, thank you for your trust and patience during what has been the hardest period of my life.

Gabriela Campos, you have been such a loyal, generous friend since we first met that I feel blessed to have you as my cómplice y confidente. Gracias, amiga.

I would also like to thank my writer friends, whom I deeply admire and respect and who have been incredibly generous in offering me, and this book, their words of support. Muchas gracias to Beatriz Hausner, Hugh Hazelton, Pura López Colomé, Hugh Hazelton, Gilbert Reid and Néstor Rodríguez for your kind words, your generosity, and your confidence in my work. I'm in your debt.

After the passing of my mother in February 2017 I found it extremely challenging to focus. I was very lucky, however, to have those people who are closest to me offering support and encouragement as I struggled to regain a sense of normalcy, not only as a writer but as a human being. I need to thank my friends for their sweetness and solidarity. Miriam López Villegas, gracias por siempre estar conmigo, por tu cariño y por echarme porras. José Antonio Villalobos and Juan Gavasa, gracias por la complicidad. Don and Jan Cross, thanks for your constant love and support, you're amazing. To all my friends near and far, thank you for holding me close to you and giving me strength.

And last, but not least, I need to thank my family.

Mamá, gracias por haber sido tan grande ejemplo de disciplina y profesionalismo. Si pude terminar este libro es gracias a lo que aprendí de ti. Te voy a extrañar siempre.

Enano, gracias por sostener el fuerte allá, para que yo pueda hacer cosas – como este libro – acá.

Pigo, gracias por tu apoyo y por tu amor constantes. Eres mi faro.

Edgar, love of my life, thank you for your loyalty, your patience, and your love. Without your support, I wouldn't have achieved anything. Te amo.

And I also want to thank my beloved children, Ivana, Natalia, and Marco, for their patience when I work. You make me happy every day and I love you more than anything.